'I'm trying to be honest with you,' he said huskily. 'That's all. There's something between us—a chemistry, a physical attraction. You know it as well as I do. And for someone who keeps work and play separate, as I do, it's both unexpec_____OK?'

Never in he_____ really believed Bl_____er. She stared up at_____attraction?

Kim swallowed hard. 'I agree. My ethics happen to be the same as yours.'

'Right. Well, it's good it's out in the open and we can deal with it,' he said softly. But he still hadn't let go of her, and his eyes had fastened on her mouth.

'Exactly.' She nodded shakily, her heart beating so hard it hurt.

'Kim…' His head descended very slowly, his eyes moving to hers.

She knew she ought to step back, to jerk her head away—something. But she didn't. She wanted him to kiss her. She didn't think beyond that.

**Helen Brooks** lives in Northamptonshire, and is married with three children and three beautiful grandchildren. As she is a committed Christian, busy housewife, mother and grandma, her spare time is at a premium, but her hobbies include reading, swimming and gardening, and walks with her husband and their Irish terrier. Her long-cherished aspiration to write became a reality when she put pen to paper on reaching the age of forty and sent the result off to Mills & Boon®.

# THE BOSS'S
# INEXPERIENCED
# SECRETARY

BY
HELEN BROOKS

⊚™ MILLS & BOON®
*Pure reading pleasure*™

First published in Great Britain 2009
Harlequin Mills & Boon Limited,
Eton House, 18-24 Paradise Road, Richmond, Surrey TW9 1SR

© Helen Brooks 2009

ISBN: 978 0 263 87225 5

Set in Times Roman 10½ on 13 pt
01-0709-50294

Printed and bound in Spain
by Litografia Rosés, S.A., Barcelona

# THE BOSS'S
# INEXPERIENCED
# SECRETARY

# CHAPTER ONE

WHY, oh, why had she been so *stupid* as to let herself in for this? The old adage of pride going before a fall was going to be borne out today; she should have backed out long before this. A polite letter saying she'd changed her mind due to un-foreseen circumstances would have done it, anything…

Kim groaned softly, staring at her reflection in the full-length mirror in her bedroom. She didn't normally inspect herself so thoroughly—usually a quick check to make sure her make-up wasn't smudged or her tights snagged was sufficient. Today was different. Today she had to appear perfectly coiffured and immaculate from the top of her head to the tips of her toes.

Deep brown eyes under a thick fringe of golden-brown hair looked anxiously back at her, before travelling the length of her body. Perhaps she shouldn't have gone for the cornflower-blue skirt and jacket? A suit in one of the more subdued colours she normally favoured would have been better. Greys and charcoals had the effect of neutralising her somewhat generous curves without emphasising that, at six foot in her stockinged feet, she was what her father kindly called statuesque. Her mother, a petite little blonde who was slender and fluttery, usually just sighed when she looked at her. The cute little baby girl her mother had insisted on dressing in lace and frills had rapidly grown into an accident-prone tomboy, and then just kept growing. She didn't think her mother had ever really forgiven her.

She brought her mind back to the cornflower-blue suit. It was too late to change; it'd have to do. She grimaced at the face in the mirror. She couldn't be late for her interview with Blaise West.

*Blaise West.* Her stomach turned over and she swallowed hard. The feeling of panic wasn't a new one; she'd been like a cat on a hot tin roof since she'd received the expensively headed letter ten days ago. It had been short and to the point. Her letter of application for the post of personal assistant to Mr West had achieved an interview at ten o'clock on the first of June at the head office of West International. There had been a number to call if the time and day were not convenient.

And she hadn't. She groaned again. Because of Kate Campion. Beautiful, cool, slim Kate, who was secretary to the manager of the accounts department and who'd labelled her Amazon Abbott. And not in a complimentary way. Oh, no, definitely not in a complimentary way.

Kim's soft mouth pulled tight. Kate and her cronies hadn't known she was occupying one of the cubicles in the ladies' cloakroom when they had breezed in to repair their make-up before going off to lunch one day some weeks ago. They'd been giggling as they'd walked in, and then she heard one of the girls say, 'Are you sure *he's* dumped *her*, Kate? It might be the other way round.'

'What? Someone as drop-dead gorgeous as Peter

Tierman being dumped by Amazon Abbott? I don't think so, Shirley. Anyway, he told me himself, after he'd asked me out to dinner tonight.'

'Really?' There had been a chorus of shrieks. 'You're going out with Peter tonight?'

'He said he'd wanted to ask me for ages but he didn't know how to let the amazon down gently. She might be ten feet tall but she's as clingy as a grapevine apparently. He felt sorry for her, that's the only reason he asked her out in the first place. Anyway, come on, I'm starving. Let's go and eat.'

They had clattered out on their stiletto heels, leaving a sickly cloud of several different perfumes in their wake by the time she'd emerged, cheeks burning and eyes flashing.

How dared they discuss her like that? And Peter, telling Kate all those lies! It had been her who'd finished with him a couple of nights before when she had finally decided she couldn't stand listening to his big ideas about himself one more time.

Handsome Peter might be, conceited he definitely was. What with his wandering hands and increasing determination to get her into bed, she had had enough. She should have ended it much sooner. She'd known on their second date that he wasn't the sort of man she'd thought he was, but she had refused so many invitations from this man or that over the last couple of years since David, she had thought she would persevere. Big mistake. Colossal.

She had gone back to her office and brooded all lunchtime as to what to do or say while she'd eaten her sandwiches. She had decided in the end not to give credence to Peter's lies by attempting to justify herself. The opportunity to put matters straight would arise sooner or later, and then she'd make sure she did it coolly, calmly and with dignity.

The nickname—which clearly was not a new thing—she could do nothing about. She had always known Kate didn't like her, probably because she had never expressed any desire to be part of her poisonous little clique.

The very next day she'd heard on the office grapevine that Kate was applying for the jewel-in-the-crown job which had been advertised both within and without West International. Personal assistant to the great man himself, Blaise West. And something, some little gremlin deep inside, had reared up and declared she was as good as Kate Campion any day, so why didn't she try for it too?

She had. She had worked on her letter of application and CV half the night and then submitted it the next morning, only to regret it immediately until she'd convinced herself she'd never hear anything about it anyway. The most that would happen was that one of those 'thank you for your application for the post of whatever. It has not been successful in this instance' letters would pop through her letterbox.

Kim took a steadying breath, turning away from the mirror and picking up her handbag. She had never been to the head office, which was located in a super-deluxe building not far from Hyde Park. West International had branches all over England as well as America and Europe, and she had worked in the Surrey division for nearly two years as secretary to the sales director. Before that, on leaving university she had had a fairly mediocre job which she'd seen as a stop gap until she married David and they started a family. Her dreams had been centred around David since they'd met at a barbeque in the first week of university life.

*Stupid.* She closed the door of the bedroom behind her. She'd had to learn the hard way that men said one thing and did another, that they weren't to be trusted.

She had to get going; she couldn't afford to be late. Nevertheless she paused in the small sunlit hall, glancing around her. She had moved into this tiny flat courtesy of getting the job at West International when her salary had doubled in one fell swoop and had never regretted it. Before that she had still lived with her parents because she had been saving hard for her wedding.

Kim loved her home. She nodded to the thought. She could walk to the office from here in fifteen minutes if she didn't want to drive, and she had a terrific boss in Alan Goode. She had plenty of good friends and a fairly active social life; one or two girlfriends had got married in the last little while but there were plenty of others who were single and enjoying themselves. She was content.

She opened the front door, stepping into the large vestibule of the tall Victorian house which had a flat on each of its three floors.

Not happy exactly—she walked to the main door, exiting into the quiet street beyond—but after the trauma of the time when David had left her and she'd thought she'd never experience peace of mind again, content would do.

And there would be no more attempts at trying to be 'normal', as her mother put it—anyone who wasn't married by the time they were twenty-five or at least in a serious relationship that was going somewhere was dubbed abnormal by her mother. She wouldn't make a mistake like Peter again.

Kim walked over to her little Mini, which was waiting for her in the street outside. There were benefits to being autonomous. She was able to please herself what she did and when she did it and with whom. No more standing in the rain on a windy Saturday afternoon watching a football match she didn't want to see. Her Saturdays with David had been a litany of those. No more putting someone else first constantly. No more allowing someone to turn a good day bad simply because they were in a disagreeable mood. The list was endless.

Why was she thinking about David so much today? she asked herself as she climbed into her car. He rarely crossed her mind from one week to the next these days. When she did think of him it was with a feeling of thankfulness for the narrow escape she'd had. The man she had thought he was would never have treated her as cruelly as David had done; she hadn't known him at all and she had been forced to acknowledge that in the weeks and months after he had walked out on her. That had been scary in itself and more than a little humiliating, but it had taught her a valuable lesson: no one ever really knew what another person was thinking or feeling, however transparent they appeared.

She started the engine, straightening her shoulders and lifting her chin. Time to drive to the railway station and then make the journey into the city. She would acquit herself as well as she could at the interview and then put the whole sorry episode behind her.

And at least she had been offered an interview. A small smile touched her lips. According to one of the other girls, Kate had been gutted when she had heard about it, having failed to secure one herself. That had been, oh, so sweet. The smile widened into an unrepentant grin as she drove off.

* * *

An hour and a half later she was sitting in the office of Blaise West's present secretary, an attractive young woman who was enormously pregnant. She had arrived a little early, just as another interviewee had been about to go into the inner sanctum. This woman had been tall and slim and beautifully dressed, with a hundred-watt smile she'd kept for Mr West's secretary. Kim she had looked up and down, her face portraying the fact she didn't think she needed worry about the competition.

Kim agreed with her. Surprisingly, it helped her nerves. She was probably the wild card in the ensemble, and if the gossip about the dynamo who was Blaise West was true, he'd realise this immediately he set eyes on her. She expected only a very short interview.

The office building was all lush carpets and glass lifts, as befitted an entrepreneur of Blaise West's standing. She'd done a little research after applying for the job. Apparently Blaise West had diversified into various money-making stratas after making his first million or two in property when he'd barely been out of short trousers. His other main forte—the manufacture and distribution of commercial and home soft furnishings—was known throughout the western world as second to none.

Kim had never even seen a picture of him, but she knew what to expect from company gossip. He was nearly forty years old, a powerhouse of energy who had a reputation for ruthlessness and cold-blooded tenacity that was legendary. He'd been married and divorced. One child. Umpteen girlfriends. Attractive, rumour had it, but then there would be plenty of women who found power and wealth attractive whatever the man in question looked like physically.

Her thoughts sped on as she pretended to flick through the glossy magazine which was one of many on the low coffee-table in front of her. The secretary had asked her if she'd like coffee when she'd first arrived, ordering it by telephone. Kim had been impressed. Blaise West's secretary and personal assistant didn't stoop to such mundane duties, then.

She'd been even more in awe when a tray had arrived almost instantly, holding a cup of coffee in an elegant, wafer-thin cup and a small plate of expensive-looking iced biscuits. It made the tea and coffee machines in the Surrey division with their paper cups and murky charcoal contents even less palatable.

She'd barely taken more than two sips of the coffee, which had proved to be scalding hot, before the hundred-watt woman emerged with a flounce from the inner office. Kim got the impression the interview hadn't gone too well. The lady in question didn't stop to exchange pleasantries with Mr West's secretary, marching straight out of the office with her head held high and her cheeks burning.

A moment after the door had closed behind her, a buzzer on the secretary's desk sounded. 'Pat?' It was a deep voice, throbbing with irritation. 'I thought you said you'd picked the best of the bunch from the applications? If what I've seen thus far is the best, I hate to think what the others were like. I trust there'll prove to be at least one who isn't completely moronic.'

Kim saw the woman glance swiftly at her as she hastily pressed a button and murmured something about 'highly qualified' into the receiver she'd picked up. Now, she couldn't hear what was being said at the other end, but after a moment or two the secretary spoke in such a low voice Kim had to strain her ears while keeping her eyes on the magazine. 'One more this morning and then one this afternoon; we agreed on half a dozen, remember? And Miss Abbott is already here.'

Another pause, and then, 'Yes, I'll do that. And I've organised the conference with the McBain people for a week on Monday, which will give our sales team time to get their presentation spot-on. You're aware your lunch engagement is one o'clock?' Replacing the receiver, the woman said to Kim, 'Mr West will see you now, Miss Abbott.'

'Thank you.' Kim stood to her feet and, as their eyes met, she said with a smile, 'I'll try and restore his faith in womankind, shall I?' It was useless trying to pretend she hadn't heard.

The secretary smiled back ruefully. 'Two of the applicants yesterday were men and they fared no better. Mr West can be a little difficult to please.'

Mr West sounded *impossible* to please. Kim kept her thoughts to herself, merely inclining her head and then waiting as the other woman tapped on the interconnecting door, opening it and standing aside for her to pass through as she said, 'Miss Abbott, Mr West.'

Stepping into the room, Kim was aware of several things seemingly all at once. Her surroundings were large and light and airy, the floor-to-ceiling windows, which took up most of the end wall, showing an incredible view of the city. The room was beautifully furnished, but then it would be. And it was quiet. Although the offices were located on an extremely busy main road, you'd never have thought it. Lastly, but not least, the bright light streaming in through the windows had the effect of turning the man sitting at the massive desk in front of her virtually into a silhouette, putting anyone entering the room at a distinct disadvantage. Something, Kim felt sure, Blaise West was fully aware of.

'Good morning, Miss Abbott. Please be seated.' He had stood to his feet as she approached, leaning forward and shaking her hand before indicating the chair placed at an angle to one side of the desk.

Kim was glad she could sit down. If the room was impressive, the man was more so. Now she could focus properly she could see he looked hard and rugged, not good-looking exactly but the thick black hair turning grey at the temples and startlingly blue eyes gave an impression of vibrant virility. He was expensively put together, his suit and shirt screaming a designer label, but it was the way the clothes sat on the big male body that was electrifying, that and his height. Probably because she was so sensitive about normally being on an eyeline or looking down an inch or two on most men, the fact that Blaise West was at least six or seven inches taller than her had come as a shock, that and the aggressive masculinity. Ridiculously it seemed wrong that he was sitting in an office. He should be scaling an unscalable mountain or fighting man-eating crocodiles in some remote undiscovered land; something extreme anyway.

Without any preliminaries whatsoever, he settled back in his huge leather chair and said coolly, 'So you want to come and work for me, Miss Abbott. Why is that?'

Coherent thought went out of the window. For the first

time in her life Kim felt she knew what a rabbit experienced when it was caught in the glare of a car's headlights. She stared at him blankly, knowing she had to say something, especially because she was confirming his earlier words—another moron.

Pulling herself together with some difficulty, she forced herself to answer the question she had expected to be asked at some point in the interview and for which she'd prepared a reply. 'As I explained in my letter, I've been at the Surrey branch for a couple of years now and feel that has given me a good grounding as to what makes West International such a hugely successful company. I like my job there but I feel it is time for more of a challenge.'

He said nothing for a few moments. Kim felt the urge to start babbling but restrained herself. Whatever she said or did she wouldn't be offered this job, she knew that, but she would like to get through this interview without making an absolute fool of herself. So instead of giving in to the nerves that were attacking her, she waited.

'Textbook answer.' It was not laudatory. 'And said in slightly different ways by the previous applicants.'

Kim decided she didn't like Blaise West. 'I'm sorry.'

'Don't be sorry, just say something original.'

She didn't think he would like the original thought that sprang to mind. Reminding herself that she certainly needed the job in Surrey and he was the controlling force in all the branches, she said stiffly, 'I would like the opportunity for more responsibility and to travel now and again, which I understand the post of your personal assistant involves.'

'Would it surprise you to know that they've all said that too?'

She definitely didn't like this man. 'Actually, no, it wouldn't.'

'Oh, and why is that?'

'Because if you treat people as morons they are likely to behave as morons,' she said sharply. She regretted it immediately, not so much for herself but because she realised too late she might have got his secretary into trouble. And one didn't answer Blaise West back; his face said so. She waited for the explosion.

'Ah…' He leaned forward, the vivid blue eyes never leaving her face. 'You heard.'

It was no good denying it. She nodded, deciding she wasn't going to apologise for her tone. If she got the sack in Surrey, she got the sack. She'd survive.

'Then I apologise. I should imagine it wasn't the best start to a job interview,' he said quietly.

The apology was so unexpected she blinked in surprise. Clearing her throat, she said warily, 'It doesn't matter, Mr West. Like the others, I am clearly not what you're looking for. Thank you for your time.' As she stood up she saw his eyes narrow.

'Where do you think you're going?'

She stared at him, her cheeks burning. 'I presumed the interview was at an end.'

'Then you presumed wrong. We haven't even started.' As she sank down in the seat again, he continued to dissect her face. She didn't think she had ever felt quite so uncomfortable in her life. 'Now…' he leant back in the leather chair once more, his elbows on the padded arm rest '…I'm going to ask that question again and I'd like a truthful answer this time. Why do you want to come and work for me, Miss Abbott?'

She couldn't remember the last time she had blushed like this. 'It was a truthful answer,' she said tightly. And then, as the black eyebrows rose quizzically, she added, 'Just not a complete one, perhaps.'

She thought she saw his mouth twitch. It was a well-shaped mouth, firm, sensual, above a cleft chin. 'So?'

His soft, silky tone didn't fool Kim. He was determined to have his pound of flesh, she thought hotly. Of course, she could make up a hundred and one things which would be more acceptable than the truth, but somehow she felt he'd know if she did. Pride straightened her spine. 'Like I said, I do feel I've gone as far as I can at your Surrey branch, but to be fair I probably wouldn't have applied for this post but for something I overheard.' She hesitated. 'Something which prompted me to step out of my comfort zone and prove something to myself, I suppose.'

The blue eyes were like lasers. 'What did you hear?'

'It was personal,' she said flatly. 'Let's just say it was aimed at me and it wasn't complimentary.'

'Anything to do with your work?'

That was a fair question in the circumstances. 'No, my work has always been satisfactory, as I'm sure Mr Goode would confirm.'

'He already has or you wouldn't be here now.' It was dry. 'So, Miss Abbott—' he paused for a moment '—are you wasting my time?'

'What?' The colour which had begun to subside flooded her cheeks again.

'Have you any intention of accepting this post should it be offered to you?'

A few minutes ago, perhaps even one minute ago, the honest answer to that question would have been no. Now…she wasn't sure. Working for someone like Blaise West would undoubtedly be terrifying and exhausting, but did she really want to stagnate in Surrey for the next ten, twenty years? And that was what she had been doing, she thought with a painful dose of self-analysis. She had a degree of independence but she was still in the comfortable cocoon of being close to family with all her friends about her. She had her job down to a fine art, there was no challenge there, and she knew exactly what she was doing from one week to the next. And that had been fine at first, in the initial fallout after David. It had been fine until she had walked into this room, in fact. 'Yes, Mr. West,' she said firmly. 'I'd consider the post, should it be offered.'

He nodded. 'Good.' At last his gaze left her and transferred to the papers on the desk. 'Then let's get on with it, shall we?'

# CHAPTER TWO

BY THE time she got home mid-afternoon, Kim felt like a wet rag. The interview with Blaise West had lasted for well over an hour and it had been gruelling. That was the only word for it. She had all but staggered out of his office, and she must have looked just as she felt because his secretary had quickly pointed out that the firm's restaurant was already serving early lunch and the food was very nice.

It had been nice, and the two cups of hot, sweet coffee she had swallowed along with roast chicken with all the trimmings had gone some way to reviving her for the journey home. She hadn't rushed over the meal, watching the other occupants of the sparklingly clean eatery while she tried to make sense of her jumbled recollections of the last hour.

The overall conclusion she came to was that she was stark, staring mad. Mad to think Blaise West might offer her the job. Mad to think she could do it if he did. She was out of her league here; way, way out. Needles of panic were making themselves felt now.

He had finished the meeting by stating he would come to a decision about the applicants within the next twenty-four hours when he had interviewed everyone. By then she had been so frazzled she'd had no idea how she had fared. Certainly hundred-watt smile had only been in with him for ten, fifteen minutes at the most, but there was another person he had to see this afternoon.

When she had finally exited West International the sunshine of early morning had given way to a grey sky that promised rain before nightfall. The train home had been delayed, and when she had eventually boarded it thousands—or so it seemed—of irritable commuters had got on with her. They had only travelled for fifteen minutes when debris on the line had meant another delay.

On reaching her home station, she had seen her little Mini faithfully waiting for her in the car park and had had to bite back tears. That alone told her she was exhausted.

Kim walked into the flat, dropping her handbag on the floor by the sofa as she collapsed into its plump depths. All the excitement and glamour of Blaise West's fast-moving world was gone. A journey that should have taken less than an hour had taken three times as long. It reminded her of something he'd pointed out during the interview.

'I'm sure you're aware of what working as my personal assistant involves, but let me spell it out anyway. I need a PA who thrives on hard work and using their own initiative, Miss Abbott. The more routine secretarial work will be delegated by you to others, but you will be required to take care of the sensitive, confidential side of things. This will involve drafting letters, reports, memos and so on, collecting and collating information for me, taking minutes, greeting and helping to entertain business contacts, organising meetings and conferences, having discussions with other PAs or customers and clients, possibly even supervising other staff on occasion. I expect absolute loyalty as well as discretion. It's essential you're capable of adapting to the needs of the job. This will mean late nights and early mornings when necessary. Is this a problem?'

She remembered she had shaken her head, feeling stunned. It was then he had added, 'I don't expect my personal assistant to be a yes-man, or -woman. But when you disagree with me you do it in private when it's just the two of us. Is that clear?' She'd nodded then, equally stunned.

Kim glanced round her sitting room. Before she had moved in she'd had the flat decorated from top to bottom exactly how she had wanted it. With her savings she had lashed out on ankle-deep carpeting, cream leather sofas and thin, drifty drapes which had been wildly expensive considering there was hardly anything to them. A new bathroom and kitchen had completed her extravagance, and her bedroom was unrepentantly feminine, soft pinks, creams and gentle mauves creating a soothing place which declared quite loudly no man lived here. And she loved it. Every inch of it. Could she continue to live here if—by the remotest chance—Blaise West offered the job to her? If the journey home was a taste of things to come…

*Stop it.* She was doing the negative thing; she always reacted like this when she was tired. The journey into London had been as smooth as silk, the return was merely bad luck. Besides which, she was getting herself all worked up for nothing. She didn't even know if she would be offered the job; there must be other applicants far more qualified and experienced than she.

And if she *was* successful? A curl of something potent stirred in the pit of her stomach. She stood up, walking into the kitchen and switching on the coffee machine. She would cross that bridge in the unlikely event she came to it.

Kim went to bed early and slept badly in spite of having tossed and turned the night before. At six in the morning she abandoned any thought of sleep, padding through into the tiny kitchen and making a mug of coffee which she drank curled up on one of the two sofas in the sitting room. She had opened the windows to the warm summer morning and shafts of sunlight and birdsong filtered into the room.

It was peaceful and cosy…but suddenly not enough. Kim sat up straighter, startled at the way her mind had gone. But it was true. Something had changed yesterday; she wasn't quite sure what or how, but the interview with Blaise West had brought to the surface a whole host of things she had been avoiding for some time.

She was only twenty-five, for goodness' sake, twenty-six in October, and she wanted to *do* something with her life. The last couple of years had been a period of licking her wounds and that was fine, but she didn't want to carry on as she had been doing. Getting the interview against all the odds had restored a smidgen of the self-confidence that had been so badly knocked when David had left her. And now the whole marriage and kids and roses round the door scenario wasn't on the agenda, she could concentrate on something she'd never envisaged having—a career.

OK, she acknowledged in the next moment, it wasn't actually the path she'd have chosen but it would have compensations. She nodded to the thought, her eyes contemplative. Broadening her horizons, travelling, meeting new people.

*Like Blaise West?* a separate part of her mind asked.

As though someone else had asked the question she spoke out loud, 'Don't be ridiculous.' She hadn't been thinking of him specifically, she *hadn't*.

*But he was the most fascinating man she had ever met in her life.* This time she didn't bother to deny it; she couldn't. It was true. She sprang up and marched into the kitchen for a second mug of coffee.

Once again established on the sofa, she took stock. Yes, Blaise West was something else but it wasn't only she who thought that. When she had gone for the interview she had already been aware of his reputation and history, both of which spoke for themselves. He was one of those rare men who had something akin to a magnetic field around them to which other people would be irresistibly drawn, whether they liked him or not.

*Did she like him?*

She considered the question. She wasn't sure. He would certainly be interesting to work for, she thought wryly. If she survived the first day, that was. But she was unlikely to get the chance. And that didn't matter, it *didn't*, because if nothing else the last twenty-four hours had told her that the next stage of her life was due to begin and it would be one in which she made changes. Changes *she* controlled. There had been enough of the other kind.

She inhaled the fragrant scent of coffee beans as she let her mind meander back into the past. She had been so gullible when she'd met David, so thrilled that someone like him—handsome, self-assured, popular—had singled her out. Her childhood had been happy enough on the whole, but her teenage years had been made miserable by her height. Or rather her sensitivity about it. She had always been the wallflower at school discos; the girl most boys avoided because she tended to tower over them. Some wit had dubbed her the beanpole when she was thirteen and the nickname had stuck for a long time, even when she had filled out in all the right places.

And then at eighteen she'd met David Stewart. Six feet three in his bare feet, blond and beautiful. An Adonis. They had been together all through university and he had proposed to her on graduation day. Her cup had been full. They'd decided while he continued to study law—his father had his own law firm which one day David would take over—she would get a nine-to-five job with no commitments so she could fit in with him and see him when he had any free time between studying at law college. He had sailed through the solicitors' final examination at the end of twelve months, and joined his father's firm to serve articles, at which time they had set the wedding date.

Every weekend she had travelled from her parents' home in Surrey to Oxford, where David lived in his family's massive seven-bedroomed house complete with swimming pool and tennis courts. His parents and younger sister adored her, and she them. Everything in the garden was rosy. And then, six weeks before the wedding, he had turned up on her doorstep one night and taken her out for a meal so they could 'talk'.

She had known even before he told her that something was dreadfully wrong but nothing could have prepared her for what she was about to hear. There was someone else. They'd only known each other a short time but it was the real thing.

Reeling from shock, she had asked who it was. Miranda,

the girl next door who had been mad about him for ever, according to what his sister had whispered? Someone at his father's work? A mutual friend?

No, he'd replied. She didn't know Francis; neither did his family.

Frances? she'd repeated shakily. Where had he met her?

It was then he had looked at her steadily and told her that the 'her' was a 'him'. It was Francis with an *I*. And he'd met him at one of the bars they both frequented. He had thought he could do the marriage and children bit to keep his family happy but he couldn't. He liked her, he assured her. Loved her even, but not in *that* way.

She had been so dumbfounded she hadn't been able to speak for some moments. And then she had got up and walked out into the pub car park, where she'd phoned for a taxi. She might have been able to follow through on the dignified and calm bit if he hadn't made the mistake of following her and trying to justify the lies and deceit of four and a half years, at which point she had shouted and screamed and finally walked across to the sports car his father had bought him for the first he'd got at university and kicked it so hard she'd dented the door. Fortunately the taxi had arrived then.

The next few weeks had been the worst of her life. Both sets of parents had been beside themselves, the brides-maids had been heartbroken they weren't going to get to wear the fairy-tale dresses which had cost a small fortune, all the wedding presents had had to be returned and the re-ception and all the other paraphernalia connected with a huge wedding cancelled.

In the midst of it all she had talked to David several

times. Although she felt he was sorry that he had hurt her, she sensed a great feeling of relief and even joy that everything was out in the open. And of course he had his Francis, with whom he had promptly set up a home in the flat they should have been renting together. He had admitted he'd cheated on her numerous times before but they had just been 'little flings'.

Kim had hardly been able to believe what she was hearing. The man she had thought she was going to spend the rest of her life with, whom she'd known and trusted implicitly for over four years, didn't exist. She had been absolutely faithful to him, refusing even a Christmas kiss at work because she felt it took something away from David, and all the time…

A hundred and one things suddenly fell into place the more she thought about it, the chief one being the reason David had never tried to get her into bed. He had talked a lot about honouring her, that he wanted his wife and the mother of his children to be different from all the rest, that, although it was terribly hard to stop at just a kiss and a cuddle, it was the right thing to do. And she had believed him! Respected him for it.

The feeling of rejection and betrayal had cut deep, and the humiliation that had gone hand in hand with it all had caused her to lose over a stone in the first few weeks. She would have followed him to the ends of the earth and she had loved him utterly but everything had been a lie. And she hadn't sensed it, hadn't known anything was wrong. That had terrified her.

The beanpole of teenage years had reared her head again and every time she looked in the mirror she had cringed at what she saw. She had felt she was nothing, less than nothing. But eventually, with the help of family and friends, she had started to eat properly and sleep soundly and get back on an even keel. She wasn't the same, she knew she wasn't the same, and she felt sad about that, mourning the loss of the trusting, happy girl she'd once been, but she was older and wiser and she would never allow herself to love anyone again the way she had loved David.

Kim came back to herself with the realisation that the coffee was quite cold. She went into the kitchen and tipped it away, standing and looking out of the window into the street below.

It was going to be a beautiful day, she thought. And life was for living. She'd done her period of mourning for what might have been if things had been different. Now she had to get on with life.

## CHAPTER THREE

KIM felt on tenterhooks all day, so much adrenaline flooding her body that she fairly ate up the work. By five o'clock her desk was clear in spite of the backlog from the day before.

Her boss walked out to the car park with her. He had asked her that morning how she had got on; now he said ruefully, 'I'd be surprised if you don't get the job, Kim. Blaise West has a reputation for knowing a diamond when he sees one.'

'Thank you.' She smiled at him. Alan Goode was a dyed-in-the-wool family man who was devoted to his wife and three boys and they'd always had an excellent working relationship. 'But you didn't see the competition. Anyway, I'm not bothered either way.' This wasn't quite true but she'd rather walk barefoot on hot coals than admit it to anyone. She knew Kate and her cronies were taking an avid interest in events.

'Now, that might be your trump card,' Alan said musingly. 'I've only met Blaise once or twice but that was enough to know he's a man who plays by his own rules. He's never conformed and he doesn't ask for conformity in others. He's an…extraordinary individual, isn't he?'

'Oh, yes.'

They smiled at each other, linked by the knowledge of what was unsaid rather than what was spoken.

'He caught his toe with his wife though—ex-wife,' Alan continued. 'She was a free spirit in every sense of the word. Any man, any time, if rumours are to be believed. She took the child when the divorce happened but then a year later she was killed in a head-on crash. Had the kid with her at the time.'

'That's awful.' Kim hadn't known about these details.

Alan shrugged. 'The child wasn't hurt too bad from what I can remember and the accident enabled Blaise to get his daughter back. I doubt he cried any crocodile tears.'

'How long ago did that happen?'

'The accident? About four years ago, I think, maybe five. The girl's ten or thereabouts now.'

Kim nodded. For a second she had a mental picture of the hard, rugged face of the man she had met yesterday. It was a face that had seen life, but it was also a face that revealed nothing of the man behind the mask. But he must have suffered. She felt a dart of sympathy even as she acknowledged it was the last emotion a man like Blaise West would ask for or want. Curiously, for no logical reason she could think of, she felt it was somehow disloyal to be talking about him. Quietly, she said, 'Goodnight, then, Alan. Give my regards to Janice.'

'I will.'

Once in the car and driving home, Kim found herself going over and over the conversation with Alan. She was still thinking about Blaise when she entered the flat, walking immediately into the bathroom and beginning to run a warm, bubbly bath. She needed a long, hot soak. Muscles she hadn't been aware of since her teens when she had been the captain of the school's netball team—being over half a foot taller than the other girls had meant she excelled in the sport—were making themselves known. She hadn't realised how tense she had been every time the phone had rung until she'd left the building.

Had she seriously thought she might be in with a chance? She shook her head at her foolishness.

And then the phone rang.

Telling herself it was almost certainly her mother or one of her friends ringing to see if she had heard anything, she nevertheless found her heart was thudding hard enough to exit her chest as she picked up the phone. 'Hello,' she said cautiously.

'Miss Abbott?'

She'd recognise the deep, distinctly smoky voice anywhere. 'Yes?' Now her heart had jumped up into her throat.

'This is Blaise West. I'd like to offer you the job as personal assistant if you're still interested after that somewhat intensive interview yesterday.'

'You would?' The note of surprise wasn't the way hundred-watt smile would have responded. Telling herself to be more professional, Kim said quickly, 'Thank you, Mr West. I would love to accept.'

'Good. I shall be in touch with Mr Goode tomorrow.'

She knew he had heard the amazement in her voice and was amused by it. Swallowing hard, she had to sit down before she could say, 'When would you like me to start?'

'You're under a month's notice, right?'

'Yes.'

'Well, I'm sure Mr Goode will have no objection if we do away with that,' he said smoothly. 'I'd like you to have some time with Pat before she leaves and because she's expecting twins that could be sooner rather than later.'

So that was why his secretary was so huge. She thought he'd left it a bit late to advertise for a new one.

As though he'd read her mind, he continued, 'It's caught us on the hop. Twins were only confirmed a few weeks ago, and it seems they're both big babies. She seems to be growing in front of my eyes every day.'

She smiled. He couldn't quite hide the irritation this unforeseen event in his no doubt orderly and controlled life had caused. 'I see,' she said carefully.

'Her doctor has already expressed an opinion that she should be prepared to rest more than is normal, and her husband is anxious that she leaves work within the next month or so. That doesn't leave much time for her to show you the ropes.'

In other words he wasn't prepared to do so, or put up with any inconvenience. Still, she supposed that was fair. He *did* own the company after all. But poor Alan was going to be left in the lurch. It was with this in mind she said, 'If I could have a few days showing a temp the necessary, I think—'

'It's Friday tomorrow. I would like to see you at the office on Monday and I shall make this clear to Mr Goode. I'm sure he will be happy with that.'

Happy wasn't the word she would have chosen. But, as he paid Alan's salary too… 'Monday morning, then,' she said politely, wondering what she'd let herself in for. She knew from the interview that the staff at the head office started work at nine-thirty, half an hour later than in the Surrey branch, but Blaise West expected his personal assistant-cum-secretary to be at her desk an hour earlier. It meant she was going to be rising at the crack of dawn for the journey into the city, but that couldn't be helped.

'Excellent.' There was a brief pause. 'I don't stand on formality, by the way. It will be Blaise and Kim unless there are clients or other personnel present.'

She didn't think she would ever be able to call him Blaise.

'The person or persons who prompted you to apply for the job…I trust they'll be hearing the good news tomorrow?' he continued.

'What? Oh, yes,' she said quickly, surprised he'd remembered.

'Then savour the moment, Kim,' he said softly. 'There won't be too many of them in life, which makes the ones that come along all the sweeter. Goodnight.'

She heard the phone click even as she murmured, 'Goodnight, Mr West,' back.

She thought of Blaise the next day. As luck would have it, she arrived at the office building just as Kate and one of her entourage walked in and they followed her into the lift. She nodded at them but said nothing, but after a moment the girl with Kate glanced at her leader before saying to Kim, 'You won't get it, you know.'

Kim had heard her quite clearly but raised her eyebrows, her tone cool as she said, 'I'm sorry? Are you talking to me?'

'The job as Blaise West's personal assistant. You haven't got a hope. Kate knows someone at Head Office and they said all the other applicants had qualifications coming out of their ears. It was a fluke you got an interview in the first place if you ask me.'

'I didn't.' Kim smiled sweetly. 'But thanks for the concern.'

'No, well, just don't get your hopes up, that's all.'

Her manner had clearly deflated the other girl. She again glanced at Kate, who, just as the lift came to a halt, said coldly, 'Personally I'd prefer to avoid the humiliation of an interview where I was clearly out of my depth.'

'Then it's fortunate you didn't get that far when you applied, isn't it?' Kim's heart was pounding like a sledge-hammer at the overt aggressiveness but it didn't show. As the lift doors opened she turned to Kate's crony, keeping her voice pleasant as she said, 'Anyway, don't worry about me. Mr West phoned last night and offered me the job, so all's well that ends well.'

She sailed out of the lift, knowing she would remember their expressions for the rest of her life. Blaise West was right. Such moments were sweet.

Kim had to keep reminding herself of that over the weekend as she oscillated between moments of euphoria and blind, unadulterated panic. She hadn't hyped anything up, she told herself umpteen times an hour. Blaise West knew exactly what he was getting. She definitely *didn't* have qualifications coming out of her ears, just a fairly respectable 2:1 degree in business studies and some years of experience. She had been honest and straightforward, even to the point of telling him she had taken business studies at university because at the time she hadn't had a clue what she wanted to so with her life and it seemed a safe option.

'Safe option?' he'd drawled. 'I don't see you as someone who would settle for the safe option.'

She had thought about that for some moments before she'd said, 'That was seven years ago.'

'Ah…' Just one syllable but she'd had the feeling he'd understood more than she would have liked.

Her mother had been cautiously enthusiastic when she'd told her parents the news over Sunday lunch. 'That's nice, dear, but don't let the job become the be-all and end-all,' she'd said carefully. Kim knew exactly what she meant. You came so close to being a normal woman and having a husband and family; don't let it all be for nothing.

Her father was great. 'Well done, sweetheart,' he'd said bracingly. 'I knew you'd get it and this'll be the start of something good, you mark my words. I feel it in my bones.'

Whether her father was right or not, on Sunday night—when her bed was piled high with clothes and she still couldn't come to a decision as to what to wear the next day—she told herself enough was enough. No more panicking, no more dissecting, no more *thinking*.

She hung the clothes away, tidied her shoes and bags and climbed into bed. She would pick the first clothes that came to hand in the morning and be done with it.

She was free of Kate Campion and her waspish companions; life could only get better.

At eight-thirty the next morning Kim was reminding herself of this was she stood in Pat's office, listening to Blaise's secretary outlining the normal procedure that occurred before the rest of the office staff arrived.

Blaise was already in his office. Pat admitted she didn't

really know what time their boss got to work, but in the five years she'd been working for him she had never arrived before Blaise once. He was a self-confessed workaholic, she ventured, but he never asked more of any employee than he was prepared to give himself.

All very commendable, Kim thought wryly, but at this precise moment that wasn't particularly comforting.

At twenty to nine the interconnecting door opened and Blaise appeared. By now Kim was feeling sick with nerves. The feeling of being out of her depth wasn't helped as she took in the dark man leaning nonchalantly in the doorway. He seemed even bigger and tougher than she remembered. More attractive too. He was wearing a blue shirt the same colour as his eyes and his tie was hanging loose, the first two or three buttons of his shirt undone and showing the beginnings of dark body hair.

The laser-sharp gaze swept over her. 'Hi.' It was casual, easy. 'Good journey this morning, I hope?'

'Fine, thank you.'

He nodded. 'Let's hope it lasts. I seem to remember Pat thinking she could commute from somewhere or other but within six months she was living in the city. Right, Pat?'

Pregnant and contented, Pat smiled serenely. 'And a month later I met John and within four months we were married.'

'Whirlwind courtship, I remember.' The piercingly blue eyes switched to Kim. 'I trust history isn't going to repeat itself?'

Kim occasionally had flashes of her father's quick wit. Straight-faced, she said, 'I doubt it; I'm sure John is very happy with Pat.'

Blaise stared at her for a moment before throwing his

head back and chuckling. 'You'll do,' he said, smiling, and disappeared back into his office.

Which was just as well. The brief glimpse of the man behind the tycoon had made Kim's knees weak. He was *gorgeous*, she told herself with something akin to horror, but she couldn't fall for her boss. Not on day one.

Whether something of what she was feeling showed in her face she wasn't sure, but the next moment Pat said quietly, 'He's not an easy man to work for but I wouldn't have missed a minute and I think you'll feel like that too. He's the most charismatic man I've ever met and has a succession of girlfriends that change with the wind. They only have to get a tiny bit clingy and they're history—he's strictly a love 'em and leave 'em type. I thought I was in love with him for a little while after I first started but I quickly realised it was a hundred times better to work for him than go out with him; he'd be murder to date. The only female who will ever lay claim to Blaise's heart is his daughter—he's devoted to her. Now, let's get back to those files. As I was saying…'

The rest of the day flew by. At the end of it Kim staggered to the train and sat in dumb senselessness all the way home. After a hot bath and a cold meat salad she fell into bed incredibly early and slept solidly until the alarm went off the next morning. The next four days were a repeat of the first and by the weekend she felt she couldn't have survived one more day without a break.

After sleeping most of Saturday and Sunday away, she went in to work on Monday morning feeling rested and prepared for the challenge. She fared slightly better that second week, and by the third had got a handle on most things. By the fourth week she knew she had gone up several gears and was coping fine. She was still exhausted most evenings but Pat said that went with the territory.

It was just as well she had acclimatised to life at Blaise's pace fairly quickly, because at the end of the fourth week Pat began to feel unwell. Within twenty-four hours there was a risk she could lose the babies. This didn't material-ise, but the end result of the scare was that she was hospit-alised and would remain virtually flat on her back for the rest of the pregnancy.

When Kim went to visit her with a bunch of flowers and several good novels, she found Pat in a private suite which didn't bear any resemblance to the general wards.

'Blaise insisted on footing the bill when it was discov-ered the firm's private health insurance didn't cover one or two things,' Pat confided once she had thanked Kim for the flowers and books. Considering Kim had had to negotiate the jungle of hothouse blooms the room held to reach the bed, her little offering looked rather forlorn. 'He got one of the top men in the country to look at me and then had me moved here.'

'That was generous of him.'

Pat nodded. 'It's certainly put John's mind at rest. He thinks Blaise is the best thing since sliced bread. How much it's all going to cost by the time the twins are actually born I dread to think, but Blaise is adamant it's OK.'

'You know Blaise wouldn't do anything he didn't want to do.' Kim smiled at the woman she had come to like very much in the last month. Pat had gone the extra mile in helping her slip into the job, smoothing out a hundred and one difficulties and being generous with her time and advice. 'Now, just try to relax and make the most of being waited on hand and foot. You're going to be pretty busy once the babies arrive.'

'I'm already bored out of my head.' Pat wrinkled her small nose. 'And I want you to promise me you'll call if there's anything you're not sure about.'

'Of course I will,' Kim lied. She had no intention of worrying Pat with office matters when she was supposed to be having complete rest and being kept free from any stress or anxiety. 'But I'll be fine. You've been fantastic the last few weeks and all those notes you've given me cover everything from A to Z.'

Pat had been taken ill during Thursday night and today was Sunday. Because Blaise had been tied up with organising the consultant and Pat's hospital care himself, Kim had seen little of him on the Friday. Tomorrow would be the first proper day she was alone with him in the role of personal assistant, and she was ridiculously nervous already. She knew Blaise well enough by now to know that she had to hide any tension she might be feeling from him, though. He valued self-control and a cool, calm approach to any situation above anything else.

She sat talking to Pat until John arrived fifteen minutes later and then made her excuses and left. She had driven into London when she discovered the hospital had a car park; she had enough of the train every day in the week. Humanity packed into a small space was never particularly uplifting—or fragrant.

She was just going to get into the car when she heard her name called. Her heart thudding, she swung round. 'Blaise—what are you doing here?' Stupid question, but he didn't appear to notice. In fact, for once he looked distinctly harassed. It suited him; made him appear more like the rest of the human race.

Kim just had time to notice how the black jeans and charcoal open-necked shirt he was wearing did even more for him than the immaculate business suits he wore to work, before he said, 'You're leaving, I take it?'

She nodded. 'Why?'

'I've got a couple of forms Pat needs to sign and as next week is going to be a busy one I thought I'd kill two birds and bring them myself and make sure they're looking after her properly. At the last minute Lucy wanted to come with me but she doesn't like hospitals.'

Kim nodded again. Pat had told her Blaise's daughter had been in hospital for a couple of weeks after the accident which had killed her mother. She had also hinted that the child was a bit of a handful.

'She's insisting she can wait in the car by herself, although I'd rather not leave her alone.'

Kim stared into the tough, attractive face. His daughter was ten years old in a couple of weeks' time, more than old enough to sit in a parked car and wait while her father delivered the papers, surely? 'I can wait a while with her if you like.'

In true Blaise style, there was no prevarication or asking her if he was putting her about. 'Thanks,' he said shortly. 'Come and meet her.'

He led the way to his Ferrari. It was a panther of a car, black and sleek and powerful, and always sat in the space reserved for it in the firm's car park like a dark, brooding presence. The young child sitting in the passenger seat couldn't have been more at odds with the car's aura. She looked much younger than nearly ten, seven at the most, and was tiny and fragile and as blonde as Blaise was dark.

As Blaise opened the door, saying, 'This is my new personal assistant, Lucy. Her name's Kim,' she bent and peered at the little girl, smiling widely.

'Hello, Lucy. Nice to meet you.'

The child stared back at her with enormous clear blue eyes. 'Hello,' she said reluctantly. She didn't smile back.

'Come and sit in; I won't be more than a minute or two.' Blaise took Kim's arm, moving her round the bonnet of the car and opening the driver's door. She had no option but to slide in beside Lucy, who was now eyeing her resentfully, as Blaise said, 'Kim's going to keep you company, Lucy,' and then shut the door.

Great. She turned to the child but before she could speak, Lucy muttered, 'I'm not a baby, you know.'

Kim watched Blaise disappear into the building in the wing mirror. 'I know that. You're ten in two weeks' time, aren't you?' she said brightly. 'Are you having a party?'

Ignoring this, Lucy continued, 'So you don't need to sit with me, all right? You can go.'

She wished. 'Your father asked me to wait until he comes out,' she stated calmly.

'I've told you, there's no need.'

Kim took a deep breath and let it out evenly. 'Nevertheless, I said I would.'

'I don't want you to.'

'I'm sorry but I can't help that.'

'This is my car, not yours. If I want you to get out then you have to.'

Thanks a million, Blaise. And this definitely didn't come under the job description. Looking into the angry little face, which was undeniably pretty, Kim said quietly, 'Are you always this rude, Lucy?'

Blue eyes blinked in surprise. For a moment Kim thought Blaise's daughter was going to defend herself but instead she repeated stubbornly, 'I want you to get out now.'

'Very well. I'll stand by the car until your father comes back, OK? Will that satisfy your desire to show me I'm just one of your father's employees?' She opened the car door but didn't exit immediately, saying first, 'One day you will learn that having lots of money and power should make you treat people under you, those not as fortunate, more kindly than anything else. Throwing your weight about makes you look like a spoilt, petulant brat, that's all. And that is extremely unattractive.'

She would have liked to climb out of the car with dignity but it was crouched so low to the ground it was more of a scramble. Shutting the door extra gently because what she really wanted to do was slam it hard, Kim stood by the car. Perfect. Not only would this little scenario make Blaise think she couldn't even handle a nine-year-old child, but she had insulted his daughter to boot. The apple of his eye. Wonderful start to the week.

She didn't glance down into the interior of the car before she saw him hurrying towards her. Then she slanted her eyes at Lucy, who was staring stiffly ahead, scowling.

As Blaise reached the car Kim began walking, saying over her shoulder, 'Over to you.' And you are more than welcome.

His voice, somewhat startled, followed her. 'Thanks. See you in the morning.'

Unless I get a phone call to tell me I needn't bother. But no, he wouldn't do that, not with Pat in hospital. Blaise wouldn't cut off his nose to spite his face.

Would he?

# CHAPTER FOUR

ALL evening Kim was on edge. She didn't regret saying what she had to Blaise's daughter—in fact, she thought Lucy had got away lightly—but at the same time the fact that the episode might have soured her future at West International had shown her just how much she wanted to work for Blaise.

She'd had no idea the job would prove to be quite so fascinating before she had started. She had imagined being the personal assistant of a multimillionaire wouldn't be boring, but Blaise wasn't even your normal run-of-the-mill mogul. He was larger than life in every way, a high-profile personality who mixed with others of the same ilk.

She had already seen that he was implacably business-like, very level-headed and more than a little cynical, but he had a wicked masculine charm that he used to great effect on occasion when all else failed. Altogether he was formidable, physically and every other way, and she still wasn't really sure if she actually liked him or not because she had the feeling Blaise only let you see what he wanted you to see. The real man was an enigma. And she didn't like that. After David, when she'd had to face the unwelcome truth that she had been all set to marry a man who was nothing more than an image he had projected which wasn't the real man at all, she had steered well clear of anyone her instinct had dubbed mysterious or a conundrum.

But she was only working for Blaise. She had comforted herself with that numerous times. And the job was, without a doubt, a peach.

It was a little later, as she lay relaxing in a warm, bubbly bath with a glass of wine at her elbow and a candle filling the air with the scent of magnolias, that it dawned on her the reason she was so unsettled tonight wasn't wholly due to the possible outcome of her confrontation with Blaise's daughter; it was seeing Blaise in a different light. A more…human light. She could barely equate the word vulnerable with her aggressive, dynamic boss, but he had certainly been different.

She sighed, wriggling her toes and then reaching for the glass of wine. She was going to pamper herself tonight; do a facial and paint her toenails and make sure she was perfectly groomed and on the ball when she went into work tomorrow. With Pat gone, Blaise needed her more than she needed him at the moment, she had to remember that. He couldn't abide disorder or any hint of confusion; his office had to run like clockwork. And she wasn't going to think of him or his brat of a daughter any more either. Tomorrow would come soon enough.

The next morning Kim strode into the office looking every inch Blaise's personal assistant. Her classic tailored suit, neat court shoes and immaculate appearance stated she was competent and proficient, and no one would have guessed she had a stomach full of butterflies doing the fandango.

She hadn't even reached her desk when the interconnecting door opened.

'Good morning.' As ever Blaise's tie was loose and the first few buttons of his shirt were undone. Kim had schooled herself to take this in her stride over the last four weeks. Just. 'Thanks for helping out with Lucy yesterday.'

She eyed him warily. The deep, smoky voice hadn't carried any hint of sarcasm or annoyance but you never could tell with Blaise. 'That's all right.'

'She's going through a bit of a troubled patch at the moment and yesterday wasn't a good day. Her grandmother, my ex-wife's mother, called round and Lucy is always unsettled after she's gone.'

Considering that not once in the last month had he said anything remotely personal, Kim didn't know how to react. But it wouldn't do to show that. Quickly, she said, 'It must be difficult knowing how to handle things at times. One of my close friends is in the same position. She says what she misses most since her divorce is being able to talk out a problem concerning one of the children at night and get a balanced view.' She immediately felt she'd said too much. Hastily, she added, 'Of course, every situation and every child is different.'

He was looking at her intently now. For a moment she thought he was going to make a dismissive remark and turn round and go back into his office. Instead he nodded slowly. 'She has something approaching a phobia about hospitals; it all dates back to the accident, I guess. Normally I wouldn't have dreamt of bringing her with me but

I was already in the car when she insisted on coming. She was getting upset and it seemed the lesser of two evils.' He shrugged. 'She's approaching that awkward age when she needs a mother to talk to.'

And from what Pat had revealed there was no chance of that. 'Couldn't she talk to her grandmother or someone else in the family?'

'If you met my ex-wife's mother you would see why that is impossible,' he said shortly. 'And there is no one else.' His tone suggested he felt he had said way too much and the blue eyes had iced over. 'The Massey file. Bring it in, would you? And I shall need those notes on the Brendan contract by ten o'clock.'

The brief glimpse of the real Blaise had gone; it was now very firmly work mode. Kim nodded. When the door to his office had closed she continued to stand for a moment, her thoughts racing. Did she assume the child hadn't repeated what she'd said to her? It would seem so.

She walked over to her filing cabinet, unlocked it and took out the Massey file. When she tapped at his door and walked in he was seated at his desk, his head bent over the papers spread out in front of him. He did not look up. She quietly placed the file on a corner of the desk but didn't speak, and when she was in her own office again she let out her breath in a whoosh.

So. It looked as though this day was the first one where she would be working as Blaise's personal assistant without any back-up. She so hoped it was a good one.

It was, all things considered. There were a few teething hiccups and Kim realised just how much Pat had helped when she was still ploughing through the last of the day's work at six-thirty, long after everyone else—except Blaise—had gone home. She finally finished a highly confidential and extremely interesting report on a company Blaise was considering taking over in Paris at seven o'clock, printing off a hard copy and then massaging her temples with weary hands.

'Tired?'

The voice from the doorway, soft though it was, made Kim jump. Her head shooting up, she saw Blaise watching her with a half-smile twisting his stern mouth. 'A bit,' she said with magnificent understatement. 'But I've finished the report on Delbouis you wanted.'

One black eyebrow rose quizzically. 'Are you trying to impress me?' he drawled lazily. It had been a complicated and detailed thirty-page document. 'If so, you've succeeded.'

'Not really,' she lied briskly. 'I'm just doing my job.'

He held out his hand for the report and she padded across to him in her bare feet, having taken off the court shoes once everyone had gone home. As always when she was near him the pleasant sensation of being fragile and feminine made itself felt. She didn't consider herself either so it was doubly nice to feel girlish against his great height and broad-muscled frame.

'Thanks.' He glanced swiftly through it while she cleared her desk and turned off the computer. 'I'll take this home and look at it more closely. Now, I don't know about you but I'm starving. I've got a table booked at Mansons for seven-thirty but my dinner companion can't make it. Care for something to eat before you go home? It'll save you cooking.'

She knew he had been going to have dinner with the

managing director of a rival company—who was also a friend—because she had made the reservation, but she remembered now she had put through a call from the man's secretary earlier that day. Taken aback by the invitation, she stared at him for a moment before forcing her voice to sound natural as she said, 'That would be nice, thank you.'

'Celebrate your first day at being thrown in at the deep end,' he said drily. 'I'll get my jacket.'

She should have said no. Kim dived into the tiny cloakroom off her office to check her reflection in the mirror over the washbasin. Deep brown eyes, a straight nose and a complexion clear of any smudges of the discreet makeup she wore to the office stared back at her. Her hair was still smoothly in place in the shining chignon she'd secured it in that morning and she looked the epitome of the well-dressed, efficient secretary. She knew Blaise was taking her out to dinner because his original companion had cancelled and she had been working late; it was merely a nice gesture, a little reward for hard work. And she wouldn't want it to be anything more. Not in a hundred years. She glared at the girl in the mirror.

Kim exited her small cloakroom as Blaise closed the door to his office. She could do this, she told herself firmly. This was the world she moved in now. In this deluxe league of high-flyers a boss didn't think anything of taking his personal assistant out to lunch or dinner; it was par for the course. She'd known when she accepted the position that she would be expected to host the odd dinner party, be prepared to fly halfway round the world at a minute's notice, move in circles hitherto unknown to her and work her socks off every hour of every day and then some. The incredible salary reflected all that.

She couldn't be provincial in her thinking or her attitude; she had to be cosmopolitan, sophisticated, worldly-wise. Blaise was the sort of man who only had to click his fingers to have a dozen women ready to jump into bed with him, OK, but that wasn't his problem, it was hers. He couldn't help his double—treble—portion of sex appeal. He was her boss, she was his personal assistant. That was how he would expect the tenor of the evening to progress.

He did. He was the perfect gentleman. Unfortunately the luxurious surroundings, wonderful food, excellent wine and not least Blaise in mode of charming dinner companion played havoc with Kim's equanimity. There was no deep conversation, no mention of Lucy or personal matters, but Blaise was lethal—all the more so because he was completely unaware of the effect he was having on her, Kim thought bitterly.

How come, after two years of complete sexual indifference to the male sex, she was physically attracted to her boss of all people? Peter Tierman was handsome and athletic with a body all the girls at work secretly swooned over, but even though she'd gone out with him it had been more because she'd felt she ought to get back into the swing of things than because she was attracted to him. It had been easy to rebuff his sexual advances—he hadn't made her heart beat faster or induced even the mildest thrill. In hindsight she was sure that was why he'd asked her out in the first place; he'd sensed her indifference and was piqued by it. She had been a challenge and with his looks and charm she knew Peter didn't get too many of those.

'Ah, desserts,' Blaise said with great satisfaction as the waiter presented each of them with an elaborate menu covering most desserts known to man. 'Are you a chocolate girl by any chance?'

'Who isn't?' Kim returned lightly. They were sitting at a table for two on a raised tier which ran round half of Mansons in a semicircle. It gave the more privileged diners the advantage of being able to look out on the main restaurant, but because the balcony was constructed of smoked glass to shoulder-level it was private too.

'Then I'd suggest the bitter-chocolate cherry torte. It never fails to reach the spot.' He grinned at her and the impact of his sex appeal crashed over her in a wave. 'Myself, I'm more of an apple pie and custard man, and they do a great cinnamon apple pie here.'

No doubt he recommended the chocolate torte to all his female companions. What would it be like to be wined and dined by a man like Blaise, knowing you were going to end up in bed with him at the end of a perfect evening? Kim swallowed hard. 'The chocolate torte sounds lovely.'

She had to get a grip. She was a grown woman of twenty-five, nearly twenty-six, and far too old to be in the throes of a crush, an unprofessional, doomed to disaster, *ridiculous* crush at that. Even if she wasn't his personal assistant, Blaise wouldn't look twice at her. She'd already learnt from the very efficient office grapevine that Blaise's women were beautiful, smart, rich, independent sirens who were every bit as desirable to the opposite sex as Blaise was to women. A six-foot, fairly ordinary-looking woman who had no experience of men to speak of and was—she was *so* glad Blaise was unable to read her mind—a virgin to boot, wouldn't ring his bell.

'So, you like chocolate.' Blaise surveyed her lazily. 'What else do I need to know that's not on your CV?'

'You didn't *need* to know I like chocolate,' Kim pointed out with a lightness she was proud of.

'And what about birthdays, thank yous, things like that?' he countered easily. 'Very useful information if you ask me, and absolutely necessary.' The blue eyes moved to her wine glass as he said, 'And you prefer red to white. Does that mean champagne's not to your liking?'

Kim smiled. 'Champagne's different.'

'That it is.'

'If it's a good one, of course.'

'The only sort I drink.'

Well, yes, it would be.

Whether her face showed something he took for disapproval she wasn't sure, but he leant forward slightly, his voice changing as he said, 'I wasn't born with a silver spoon in my mouth if that's what you're thinking.'

'I wasn't.' It was true.

'Good.' He took a swallow of the excellent wine, which carried an aroma of cherries and ripe blackberries. 'I know all about cheap champagne and inferior wine, but I decided early on after sampling both that if I couldn't afford the best I'd have nothing.'

Kim nodded. Her voice dry, she said, 'It must have helped that particular decision that you made good so young.'

The blue eyes crinkled and her stomach jumped. 'That's true,' he said, smiling, 'although I like to think I would have held out however long it took.'

'How old were you when you went into the property business?' He had started the personal tone to the conversation and this was something she wanted to hear about—his beginnings.

'Sixteen.' His smile widened at her surprise. 'I left school one week and started work doing up a wreck of a place with a couple of older friends the next.'

'You didn't want to stay on for further education?'

'I was a rebel all through school,' he said quietly. 'I couldn't wait to leave and the teachers couldn't wait to get rid of me. I regret it to some extent now—education is a wonderful tool to have—but maybe things wouldn't have turned out so well if I'd gone down that route. Who knows?'

'Didn't your parents try to persuade you to stay on?'

A shutter came down over his eyes. It was the only way to describe the sudden and complete withdrawal. 'I never knew my parents. I was one of those "A newborn baby has been found dumped on the steps of a hospital and the police wish to contact the mother, who they feel is in urgent need of medical attention" scenarios. I was adopted as a baby but the couple were killed in a car accident when I was three years old; I have no memory of them, although they left me their name and an inheritance which I came into when I was eighteen. I used that to buy my first own property and with the experience I'd gained since leaving school it worked out very well.' His voice was flat, controlled.

She was aghast and trying not to show it. Keeping her voice level with some difficulty, she said, 'Who looked after you when you were a child?'

'A succession of foster parents.' He shrugged. 'I wasn't

easy from day one apparently. Now, what about you? Brothers, sisters?'

It was a definite refusal to discuss himself any further. 'I'm an only child. My mother would have liked more but it didn't happen, so that was a double disappointment.'

'A double disappointment?'

She hadn't intended to say the last bit; that was the potency of the wine talking. Mentally kicking herself, Kim forced a smile. 'My mother had her heart set on a pretty little girl who would play with dolls all day, the sort of child she'd been. I—I wasn't like that.'

'No?' He leant forward again. 'What were you like?' he asked, as though he really wanted to know.

'A tomboy.' She didn't want to do this.

'And she tried to make you into something else?'

'Not really, no. I just was always aware I was…well, failing her, I suppose.'

'Because you were yourself?'

He sounded almost angry and Kim was quick to defend her mother, guilt making her voice sharp. 'She wasn't unkind, it wasn't like that. She was, she *is*, a wonderful mother. We're just different, that's all. She's small and cute and very feminine, like one of the old-style southern belles, my father always says.' She smiled but Blaise didn't smile back.

Quickly, she added, 'Like in *Gone with the Wind*, you know?'

Ignoring this, he said, 'You're very feminine.'

Oh, hell, he thought he had to compliment her now. She knew she was slowly turning bright red with mortification. Deciding the best way to finish what had turned into a highly embarrassing conversation was not to labour the point, she said brightly, 'Thank you,' and gulped at her wine.

'You don't think so?' Blaise looked as if he was not going to abandon the subject just because the other person wished they could crawl into a hole and die.

'Not particularly, no.'

When the waiter chose that moment to return with their desserts she could have kissed the man. As it was she gave him such a beaming smile he was visibly startled.

'Mmm, this is delicious.' She attacked the torte with indecent haste to deflect any return to the subject of her femininity. 'Absolutely gorgeous.'

He waited until her mouth was full again before he said, 'You are an extremely attractive, feminine woman, as any man in this place would verify.'

For a horrifying moment she thought he was going to stand up and ask for volunteers. Half choking on the torte, she mumbled again, 'Thank you,' and prayed he would leave well alone.

The torte was heavenly but her taste buds weren't doing it justice. All she wanted to do now was to escape from those intent blue eyes that, she'd noticed in the past, always seemed to see too much.

Her prayers were answered though. For the rest of the meal and over coffee Blaise reverted to amusing dinner companion, a role he'd got down to a fine art, Kim thought somewhat nastily as her hot colour began to subside. Always overly sensitive about her height and generous curves, she could not imagine what had led her to speak the way she had. And to Blaise of all people. It looked as though she had been fishing for compliments at best and had some sort of psychological hang-up at worst. And while there might be a grain of truth in the latter, she admitted fairly as she swallowed the last of her coffee, she would rather walk through the streets of London stark naked than make him feel he had to say what he had.

They emerged from Mansons's air-conditioned luxury into warm city air that carried the smell of all big cities; a mixture of petrol fumes, hot pavements, hamburger stalls and diverse humanity. 'Thank you for a lovely dinner,' Kim said quickly. 'I'll see you tomorrow morning.'

'I'll drop you off at the train station.' Blaise's car was parked a few yards away, the reason he had only had one glass of wine with the meal. She, unfortunately, had been tempted to two, Kim reminded herself. Which was why she had said too much and why she would have to take a taxi from the train station in Surrey and leave her car overnight.

'No need—it's only five minutes from here and I'd enjoy the walk after being inside all day.' The thought of sitting in that beautiful monster again was too much tonight, especially when the other occupant in this case would be Blaise himself.

He didn't argue. 'Fine.' He smiled politely. 'Goodnight, Kim.' It was pleasant, impersonal.

'Goodnight.' She turned, making her way along the pavement as carefully as though her heels were of the four-inch variety rather than the one-and-a-half she allowed herself, feeling flat shoes weren't smart enough for the office.

She had tried on a fabulous pair of vertiginous stilettos once in a shoe shop which had specialised in sexy Italian shoes. Her legs had looked endless, but unfortunately so had the rest of her, she remembered wryly. She had finished up buying another pair of low, smart court shoes. Even then she had been on a level with David when she'd worn them.

*She could buy those other shoes if she was with Blaise.*

The thought, coming from nowhere as it did, caused her to stumble. She recovered instantly and didn't glance round to see if Blaise had gone; she'd had enough self-inflicted humiliation for one day.

It was much later, when she was home and tucked up in bed and on the verge of sleep, that his words about his childhood came to mind. She didn't like to think of the tough, cynical man she knew as a hurt and confused little boy; it was too painful. And then his wife playing around—if all the rumours were right—and taking his daughter when they'd divorced. He might have the Midas touch where business was concerned but his life hadn't been easy.

Her thoughts gnawed at her for a few minutes before she purposely blanked her mind and began the relaxation exercises she'd learnt in the aftermath of David when she hadn't slept properly for weeks.

In less than five minutes she was fast asleep.

# CHAPTER FIVE

KIM dreaded going into work the next morning after Blaise had taken her for dinner, but in the event it was something of an anticlimax. The day was as hectic and fast-moving as ever, but there was no awkwardness or uncomfortableness, certainly not on Blaise's side anyway. And gradually through the morning Kim relaxed. By the time she left the building that evening she was wondering if she had imagined the whole thing! The meal with Blaise, their conversation, everything.

The week flew by at a frantic pace but it was exhilarating and fulfilling to be in such a high-powered job and to be doing it well. And she was. She knew she was. She was getting better at recognising what she could delegate and what she could not, and she found this had reduced her workload a little. And it was nice to have the office to herself, much as she had liked Pat and got on with her. She could concentrate fully on the task in hand, except on the occasions when Blaise wandered into the outer office to discuss something or other.

Kim had discovered when he was totally in work mode he would call her into his domain if something needed to be said or done, firing off orders like an automatic rifle. But now and then, if the razor-sharp mind was mulling something over or if he wanted to get a different slant on a problem, he would stroll into her office and perch himself on the edge of the desk while he talked. It didn't happen very often and for this Kim was thankful. Trousers pulled tight over taut thighs and the faint scent of his delicious aftershave was not conducive to getting through a shedload of work before evening. The trouble was, long after he'd disappeared back into his territory she would be left battling the sort of thoughts she would have sworn on oath before she'd come to work for Blaise she was incapable of.

By the weekend she wasn't quite so exhausted as in previous weeks and even managed to get round to her parents' for Sunday lunch. It wasn't terribly successful— her mother managed to weave into the conversation that two of her friends' daughters had just got engaged and dear Emmeline's daughter had just given birth to a little boy, 'such a darling little thing and Angela has taken to motherhood like a duck to water'. She had been ungracious enough to mutter she wasn't surprised; Angela had always waddled like a duck even before she was pregnant.

Monday morning was the sort of baking hot English day that promised thunderstorms and flash floods could be on the agenda before nightfall. Dressed in the thinnest summer frock she possessed that was still high enough in the bodice and low enough over the knees to be suitable for the office, Kim got onto the train, congratulating herself she'd thought to bring her umbrella.

She was two yards away from the main door of West International when she realized she'd left it propped happily to one side of her seat. Well, that was it—it would *definitely* rain later on now, she thought with a pessimistic scowl, and then nearly went headlong as the heel of her shoe caught in the crack of the pavement and snapped clean off.

*Great.* Leaving the heel where it was, she limped into the building, where Christine, the receptionist, helpfully told her that *she* always kept a spare pair of shoes at work for just such an emergency. Baring her teeth in a smile, Kim thanked her for the tip.

Once in her office she took off her shoes, flinging them under her desk. She'd try and nip out during her lunch break and buy another pair. An umbrella too, while she was about it. This was clearly going to be one of those days.

Kim realised how right she'd been when Blaise strolled out a few minutes later, a bubblegum-pink envelope in his hand. Without any preamble or 'how's your weekend been?' he perched himself on the side of the desk and looked down at her with narrowed blue eyes. 'What did you and Lucy talk about that day at the hospital?'

'What?' She was instantly on the defensive.

'When you sat with her for a while.'

She stared at him. The shimmering blue eyes gave nothing away; they never did. Well, two could play at that game. She shrugged. 'I don't remember.'

He was in dark grey trousers and a silver-grey shirt. He looked aggressively attractive. Then she realised she'd got the aggressive bit wrong when he smiled, his rugged face mellowing. 'Well, whatever it was you seem to have made an impression. She wants to invite you to her birthday party at the weekend,' he said easily, slinging the envelope onto her desk.

If it had been a grenade she couldn't have been more shocked. 'Me?'

'You.' He stood up, walking back to his office as he said over his shoulder, 'It's a casual affair. A barbeque round the swimming pool in the afternoon and then dancing to a band at night in the garden. The world and his wife are coming.'

*His* world with their wives! She wouldn't know a soul and she wasn't at all sure why Lucy wanted her there. Young girls could be spiteful; she remembered the relentless teasing she'd got at school over her height. Maybe Lucy had something in mind to—in the child's mind—bring her down a peg or two. She opened her mouth to say she was busy at the weekend, when he added, 'I've told her you're probably doing something, so don't feel obliged to come, but you're welcome if you're free.'

In other words he couldn't give a monkey's one way or the other! Ridiculous, but it rankled. It shouldn't have, but it did. Before Kim thought twice about the implications, she said, 'Actually I'm not doing anything special this weekend.' Like all the ones before it.

'Really?' Blaise turned at the door and nodded. 'I'll tell Lucy—she'll be pleased.' And then he stepped into his office and shut the door.

Stupid, stupid, stupid. Kim sat looking blankly at her computer. What on earth had possessed her?

That was easy to answer, the little gremlin who sometimes controlled her pride answered. Blaise had felt obliged to give her the invitation because his daughter has asked him to, but he'd made it pretty plain he didn't expect her to accept. For a moment all the times she'd been a wallflower at the school discos when the smoochy numbers were played, all the covert and sometimes not so covert teasing she'd endured through her early teenage years, David's betrayal and the humiliation she'd suffered and—not least—'Amazon Abbott' had risen up. She'd be blowed if she was going to put up with more rebuffs, that was what she'd thought.

Kim groaned softly. This was what being over-sensitive could lead to. Blaise hadn't been putting her down. Why should he care if his secretary came to his daughter's shindig or not? She'd been on excellent terms with Alan Goode and his wife, babysitting for them on occasion and joining them at one or two family functions, but she had always known it was basically a work friendship. Expendable. It hadn't bothered her, so why was she being so touchy now?

*Because Alan Goode was not Blaise West.*

Kim groaned again. The truth was pretty unpalatable. She had to get a handle on this whole Blaise thing because if she didn't she was in danger of spoiling a fantastic job and a once-in-a-lifetime opportunity. Once you'd worked for someone as high-powered as Blaise for a reasonable length of time, the world would be your oyster when you wanted to move on.

By mid-morning she'd given herself a thorough talking-to and felt considerably better. She had seen the effect Blaise had on other women—it wasn't only her who was disturbed by his particular brand of maleness—and so perhaps it was inevitable that working in such close contact with him would cause a few problems initially. Pat had admitted to the same. This was only a problem if she made it one.

At eleven o'clock she put a call through to Blaise from

Ross Harman, his luncheon appointment. A moment after the call finished he put his head round the door. 'Ross's assistant's gone home sick,' he said shortly. 'OK to join us so you can take notes?'

'Of course,' she answered automatically. He was just about to disappear again when her 'Oh!' stopped him.

'Problem?'

'My shoes.'

'Your shoes?'

'I don't have any. At least, I have some, of course I have some, but the heel broke off one on the way to work.' She could kick herself. Talk about unprofessional. Even the receptionist kept a spare set for emergencies.

'That's easily dealt with. Phone Marshalls and tell them to send several alternatives in your size, colour and so on.'

Marshalls? You had to be earning a fortune just to look in the window. 'I don't think—'

'They know me; there won't be a difficulty.'

Except a pair of shoes from Marshalls was likely to cost the equivalent of a month's salary! Fine if you were a footballer's wife. Still, she supposed she could afford it now with what Blaise was paying her. Kim nodded. 'It's eleven o'clock, though; we'd have to leave at twelve.'

Blaise smiled, his face amused. 'Trust me. Just phone.'

Within ten minutes the manager of Marshalls and one of his staff were laying out a dozen pairs of shoes for Kim to look at. She had never felt so embarrassed in her life, especially because Blaise strolled out of his office to add his opinion to theirs.

Painfully aware of her size-nine boats and unutterably thankful she'd had a pampering session Sunday evening and waxed her legs, painted her toenails a gorgeous cherry-red and used an expensive fake tan, Kim chose a couple of pairs of sandals and three pairs of shoes to try on. The prices were on the boxes but in such tiny print it was impossible to read them without being obvious.

One pair of sandals in the softest leather imaginable were the same pale yellow as her dress and Kim was sorely tempted. Telling herself to be sensible and choose something that would go with several outfits, she settled for a pair of cream shoes with tiny stiletto heels and a peep-toe. Bravely she smiled up at the manager. 'How much do I owe you?'

'Don't worry about that now.' Blaise glanced at his watch. 'We have to leave shortly. Send the bill here, Antonio, would you? And leave the lemon sandals too.'

Kim stared at him. What on earth was he doing? She opened her mouth to protest but Antonio and his assistant—a petite redhead who had hardly been able to take her eyes off Blaise the whole time, which Kim thought was *highly* unprofessional—had whisked up their wares and were already leaving.

As the door shut behind them, Kim stared at her boss. 'I only want one pair,' she said ungraciously. 'Now I'll have to take the sandals back tonight.'

'How do you know I meant you to keep them?'

Kim wondered how many women he knew with size nine feet who wanted a pair of lemon sandals. Giving him the benefit of the doubt, she raised her eyebrows. 'Did you?'

'Yes.'

How did you explain to a multimillionaire that one pair of shoes from Marshalls—who dealt purely with only the best designers, as the manager had been careful to point out before he was through the door—was an extravagance, but two was plain madness? 'I prefer the cream,' she said shortly.

'The lemon looked better with your dress. And stop glaring at me just because I've bought you a couple of pairs of shoes.'

It took a moment for the words to register; then her voice came low but firm when she said, 'You have not! I'm perfectly capable of buying them myself.'

'I don't doubt that, Kim, but they're a thank-you for stepping up to the mark when Pat was taken ill so suddenly. And without any fuss or commotion. I'm fully aware I can expect a lot but you've delivered.'

She went on staring at him. She had absolutely no intention of accepting such an expensive gift but it was the fact that he had said what he'd said that was so flabbergasting. He wasn't the sort of man to say thank-you. When he paid someone to do a job he would expect it would be done extremely well, end of story. At least she had thought that was what he was like.

Kim wasn't aware of the transparency of her face but the big, dark man watching her read her thoughts as clearly as if she had spoken them. With dry amusement, he said, 'OK?'

No, no, not OK. Finding her voice, Kim forced herself to say, 'It's very kind of you but I couldn't possibly accept. You pay me to do my job, Blaise.'

A touch of irritation sounded: 'I insist.'

'I'm sorry but I can't.'

For a second he frowned. 'Would you object to my buying you a Christmas box?'

'That's different, that's—' she had been about to say 'normal' but changed it to '—an accepted nicety.'

'Great. You've had your Christmas box early.'

'It's July.'

'I did say early.' He grinned at her, disappearing back into his office as he said, 'And wear the sandals today. They look perfect with that dress and your nail polish. I wouldn't have put you down as a cherry-red female.'

She had to ask. Just before he shut the door, she said, 'What would you have put me down as?'

Glittering blue eyes met hers. 'Pearl perhaps, or opal. Something soft and lustrous.'

Kim blinked.

'But the red is very nice,' he said, straight-faced, and closed the door to his office.

He was laughing at her. Kim looked down at the two pairs of shoes. But not in a nasty way. And she had five minutes to repair her make-up and compose herself into the quiet, efficient secretary she needed to be.

Lunch went without a hitch. She ate her meal, took the necessary notes as they enjoyed coffee in the lounge area of the restaurant and was careful to have no more than one small glass of wine. She had met Ross Harman before and she had liked him. He was a small, dapper man who had built up his own business empire from scratch, had a no-nonsense approach to life and work and who was still married to the woman he had met before he'd got wealthy. No mean feat in the super-rich circles he and Blaise moved in.

Was that what Blaise would have liked? Kim asked herself as the three of them left the restaurant, Ross going in one direction and they in another. The restaurant was only a short walk from the office and so they didn't need a taxi. Blaise took her elbow as they walked, moving her into the inside of the pavement with a courtesy that was completely natural and chatting away about the deal with Harmans.

Kim found it difficult to concentrate. It was a rare experience when she had heels on to physically look up at a man and she was still getting used to it with Blaise, added to which his close proximity was more than a little unnerving. It wasn't just his height and breadth that made her feel deliciously feminine and almost delicate—she snorted in her mind at the word but it was true, none the less—but the hard masculinity that was an integral part of his attraction.

David had been tall but he'd been slim, almost boyish, and very fair. He had never made her feel particularly *womanly*, she thought as she replied to something Blaise had said, and at the time she had blamed that on herself. With bitter hindsight she'd realised it was because he liked her— loved her, even—without wanting her physically. Maybe if she hadn't always had an inferiority complex about her height and big-boned figure she'd have guessed something was wrong before they had got so near to the wedding date. But then again, maybe not. She had loved and trusted him with a blind devotion that saw no wrong in the beloved. And perhaps her vulnerability in that area was why David had picked her in the first place. Who knew?

'What's the matter?'

The deep, smoky voice at the side of her brought Kim's dark brown eyes flashing to Blaise's face. For a few seconds she had lost focus; big mistake with someone as astute as Blaise. 'The matter? Nothing.'

'I sure as hell hope it's not me who's put that expression on your face. I asked you how long it would take you to get those notes done and you were glaring again.'

'I wasn't glaring,' she protested weakly. 'I was just thinking of something briefly, that's all. And the notes will be on your desk within an hour, OK?'

Blaise did not reply to this. What he did say was, and in a tone that suggested he was talking as much to himself as her, 'No, not glaring, you're right. It was more…tragic than a glare.'

'Tragic?' She bitterly resented that. 'I don't think so!'

'I do.'

To Kim's horror he stopped, taking hold of both her arms and drawing her round to face him. 'Leaving aside the little matter of you disappearing somewhere when you're supposed to be with me, I ask again, what's the matter?'

It was the normal lunchtime rush hour and very few people could get away with stopping dead on a busy London pavement without being bumped and jostled, but Blaise managed it. Kim stared up into the craggy face. Why did this man have to be her boss? she asked herself helplessly. Why couldn't she have met him years ago, before David, in one of those romantic encounters you saw so often in films? Two hearts beating faster, eyes locked, both knowing something momentous had happened…

'Now you look vacant,' Blaise said drily.

Coming back to earth with a bump, Kim forced a smile. It was either that or turn huffy and that was a luxury she couldn't afford. 'There's no pleasing you,' she said lightly.

'Now, that's where you're wrong.' The amusement had gone from his face. 'You please me, Kim, very much.'

They stared at each other for a moment and then the shutter she had seen in operation a couple of times came down over his face, but not before Kim had seen what almost looked like shock registering in the blue eyes.

He let go of her, beginning to walk again but this time without touching her, his voice as light as hers had been when he said, 'If you were leaving tomorrow in all honesty I could write "highly satisfactory" on your reference.'

What did that mean? Inwardly perturbed but determined not to show it, Kim matched her stride to his. 'That would do for a start but I'd expect "always very punctual" and "works well in all situations" and the rest of the normal waffle as well.'

'I never waffle.'

That was true. 'Not even for a reference?'

'Especially for a reference. Although to be truthful I can't remember having to write one for my personal assistants; they tend to stay the course and leave for other reasons than another job.'

She could believe that was true too. Glad to be discussing safer subjects than her thoughts, Kim asked curiously, 'How many have you had?'

They were in sight of the office building now. He glanced at her, very much the iron-hard, controlled individual she was used to. 'Three, as it happens. The first one, a feisty old soul called Nancy, was with me from the beginning and evolutionised into the job as things took off. When she retired at sixty I didn't know how I'd cope without her but she was emigrating with her daughter and family so there was no chance she could stay on any longer. It was a learning curve but a good one. I found out everyone is expendable.'

Kim blinked. Something had changed in the last minute

or so. *He* had changed. It was as though she had done something wrong.

'The second you met: Pat.'

'Right.' Kim concentrated on negotiating the section of pavement which had ripped off her heel earlier that day, and nothing more was said as they entered the air-conditioned confines of West International. The receptionist on duty gave Blaise the sycophantic smile she kept especially for him, receiving a brisk nod in return.

Once in the lift, Kim stared straight ahead. What a contradiction Blaise West was. But then that was probably what made him so attractive to the opposite sex; strength and gentleness were a potent combination in any man. And Blaise had both, even if the latter wasn't flaunted very often. Add that to his powerful masculinity and you had a combination that was positively deadly.

Seated at her desk, Kim went straight to work on the pages of notes she'd taken, delivering them to Blaise within the allotted hour. The dark head was bent to the papers strewn about his desk and he didn't look up, muttering his thanks as he frowned at something or other he was looking at. Totally in work mode.

As she reached the door, his voice brought her turning. 'I'm not happy with the time schedules in the Paris branch; I don't know what the hell Lemoine is thinking of, allowing Delbouis to dictate terms to us like this. I was hoping that Claude Lemoine could deal with this but I was mistaken. I shall need to go over myself and see Delbouis and let him know who's calling the shots. If he wants me to buy his company then he falls in line.'

'Perhaps he doesn't.'

'What?' The piercing eyes pinned hers.

'You told me Jacques Delbouis built his company up from nothing, didn't you? Perhaps at the heart of him he doesn't want anyone to buy it.'

'I'm bailing him out of certain financial ruin by doing so.' Blaise's voice was clipped; he clearly didn't appreciate her comment.

'I know that and in the circumstances it's a very generous offer.'

'Oh, thank you,' he said with heavy sarcasm. 'It's nice to know you don't think I'm stealing it away from him.'

'But nevertheless, he must feel pretty awful. Think how you'd feel if it was you.'

'I wouldn't have been so foolish as to buy stock I had no money to pay for on the hope of promised orders which did not materialise,' Blaise said crisply. 'And then further compound that mistake by taking loans with excessively high interest.'

Kim stared at him. 'Don't you feel even a tiny bit sorry for his predicament?'

'There's no room in the business world for pity. You know that. Delbouis made bad decisions and he's paying for them. It's as simple as that.' Blaise sat back in his big leather chair, his face impassive now. 'Dog eat dog, Kim. Survival of the fittest.'

When he was like this she could see what had made him a millionaire when he was barely in his twenties. He didn't seem quite human. Flushing, she said shortly, 'Yes, of course I know that. I was talking about your...personal feelings.'

'I allow myself very few "personal feelings".' His voice was deep, disturbing, and Kim felt he wasn't referring only to work now. 'I learnt a long time ago they can cloud judgement and make strong men weak. Neither is to my liking.'

She didn't know what to say. A fairly trivial conversation had turned into something else and she was out of her depth. The pause grew longer but she still couldn't find words to end it.

Bending forward again, he lowered his eyes to the papers in front of him. 'I'll go to Paris tomorrow. Make the necessary arrangements for us, will you? An overnight stay in the usual hotel should do it. Pat's left a complete list of such things for you, hasn't she?'

Kim nodded, taken up with the 'us'. 'You want me to accompany you?' she asked with a matter-of-factness she was far from feeling. She had known such trips would happen, of course; Pat had told her she'd accompanied Blaise to America and most of the branches in England and Europe.

Blaise nodded without looking at her. 'I trust that's not a problem.'

'Of course not,' she answered, her voice as crisp as his had been. 'I'll see to the arrangements at once.'

Once in the outer office Kim drew in a long, shaky breath. This *wasn't* going to be a problem. She had found her feet here now. She could take the work and social niceties a business trip to Paris would bring completely in her stride, and she had better get used to such events because it was unlikely this would be her last.

She fetched Pat's comprehensive list of hotels and other travel details out of the desk drawer and got to work, and not once did she allow herself to concede that it wasn't the work or the social niceties that had caused that host of butterflies in her stomach but the intimacy of being in Paris with Blaise.

# CHAPTER SIX

KIM was up at the crack of dawn the next morning. She had followed Pat's instructions to the letter, which meant they were booked on an early-morning flight, first class, with a car to meet them at the airport and take them to the hotel. Five-star. Naturally.

She had packed her overnight case the evening before, adding her most expensive evening dress just in case. With it being a five-star hotel she assumed folk might dress for dinner. If they didn't, she had a fine wool dress in soft cream that would do as a smart-casual option.

Once dressed, she stared at herself in the mirror. Her flowing trousers in pale green silk and wool had cost her a mint at the time but they'd been worth every penny. She'd had them for three years now and they still looked as good as the day she had bought them. Having teamed them with a sleeveless white linen blouse and a thin white linen jacket, she looked cool, professional and chic. Just the image she wanted to project. She might be as nervous as a cat on a hot tin roof but it was imperative Blaise didn't pick that up.

She normally twisted her shoulder-length hair into a knot

at the back of her head for the office, but leaving it down was more comfortable for travelling. She brushed it into a sleek golden-brown curtain falling either side of her face, tiny diamond earrings and her wristwatch her only jewellery.

She reached the airport before Blaise. They had arranged to meet in the coffee lounge and as she sat drinking her cappuccino she saw him striding across the space between them, looking big and hard and uncompromising. He was several inches taller than anyone else, dressed in a light grey suit and dusky mauve shirt and tie, and more than one pair of hungry female eyes followed his progress.

The muscles in every part of her body tightened and she told herself to relax. She had forty-eight hours of being with Blaise; she'd be a nervous wreck at the end of that time if she didn't lighten up.

'Good morning.' The sapphire gaze flashed over her and Kim felt the impact down to her toes. 'The flight's on time, so once you've finished we'll make our way through.'

'I'm ready.' She drained the last of the coffee and stood up immediately.

'Here.' Blaise had extracted a crisp white handkerchief from his pocket and reached forward, stroking the corner of her mouth. 'Foam,' he explained briefly, returning the handkerchief to his pocket. Bending down, he picked up her case and moved off.

She was glad for the time to recover herself and for the burning colour that had flooded her face to die down. It had been a simple gesture, nothing out of the ordinary, but as he'd bent towards her it had seemed more intimate than anything she'd experienced with David.

Following in Blaise's tracks, Kim discovered how the

petty inconveniences of air travel were ironed out if you could afford it. Before she knew it they were whisked up to the first-class lounge, which was in stark contrast to the busy, loud arrivals terminal they'd left. Within a short time they walked through to the plane and were settled in extremely comfortable seats with plenty of leg room.

Kim concentrated on looking out of the window, trying to ignore how Blaise's presence in the adjoining seat was affecting her equilibrium. In the bustle of sitting down, her eyes had been drawn to the tautness of his thighs, the maleness of him overwhelming in the limited confines of the plane despite the relative spaciousness of First Class.

Once they were airborne the stewardess brought the coffee they'd ordered and Blaise extracted a wad of papers from his briefcase, immediately becoming absorbed in the facts and figures they contained. Kim continued to look out of the window but her eyes weren't really seeing the outside world; her whole being was vitally aware of every movement Blaise made, each rustle of the papers and the impatient click of his tongue now and again as he examined Claude Lemoine's report.

She certainly wouldn't want to be in Claude Lemoine's shoes when the two men met shortly, she thought ruefully. She just hoped the poor man had prepared a good case for his shortcomings.

A few minutes before they landed Blaise stuffed his papers back into the briefcase and stretched lazily. 'OK?' he asked quietly, glancing at Kim as though he had only just remembered he wasn't travelling alone.

She nodded, her hair moving like oiled silk before swinging back into place. His eyes followed the movement before falling to her mouth. It was a moment before he said, 'The car will drop our things off at the hotel but I want to go straight on to Delbouis's factory. Do you need to freshen up at all?'

Straight in the deep end, then. 'No, I'm fine.'

'Claude's meeting us there. I said all I want to say to him last night on the phone.'

Oh, dear. She had a feeling this day was going to be on the stressful side.

Her face must have revealed something of what she was thinking because the stern, sensual mouth curved slightly. 'Don't worry,' he said softly. 'I won't make things too uncomfortable for you.'

She flushed at the mocking quality to the smoky voice. 'You must do as you see fit.'

'Thank you,' he said gravely. 'I shall.'

She glanced at him, forcing a small, cool smile. 'Not that you ever do anything other than that, I'm sure.'

'Is that a bad thing?'

'I didn't say that.'

'But you say so much without words,' he countered evenly. 'A glance here, a sidelong look there, and I feel like a naughty schoolboy being reprimanded.'

Kim stared at him, utterly astonished. 'I— You're my boss. I wouldn't dream of—of reprimanding you,' she stammered, hearing her faltering voice with annoyance.

'I had a headmistress who was the same,' he continued as though she hadn't spoken. 'The sergeant major we used to call her. We were all terrified of Miss Bates.'

She didn't believe Blaise West had ever been terrified of anyone or anything in his life, and she certainly didn't appreciate being compared to his old headmistress. Her tone reflected this when she said, 'I'm sure I'm nothing like your headmistress.'

'Oh, you are, Kim. I promise you. And if you knew her you'd take it as a compliment. She was quite a woman, was Miss Bates. She could control a class of tough East End tearaways without so much as raising her voice; a lift of one eyebrow would do it. She left to marry some guy who was going exploring in the wilds of Borneo or some such place, and she went with him. If anyone could quell the natives, Miss Bates could.'

She felt a little mollified Miss Bates hadn't been some ancient old hag with thin hair and a moustache. Although she still might have been, she supposed. 'Is that where you were brought up?' she asked quietly. 'The east end of London?'

'Some of the time.'

Remembering what he had said about his troubled childhood, Kim didn't probe any further. 'My parents still live in the same house where I was born in Surrey,' she proffered.

'Nice place?'

'I think so. It's not grand,' she added hastily, 'just a fairly average-size three-bedroomed house, but it's got a wonderful garden, huge, and full of trees. I used to spend most of my time outside when I was young.'

'The tomboy.' He nodded. 'I remember.'

Kim smiled. 'There's a massive weeping-willow at the bottom of the garden and it was my best friend. I even used to do my homework up high in its branches.'

He looked at her, his eyes intently searching her face. 'Were you a happy child?'

'On the whole.' She wasn't aware of the shadow that had crossed her face.

'On the whole?' he pressed softly. 'But not all the time?'

'Who's happy all the time?'

'Point taken.'

His eyes had narrowed on her face. Kim didn't quite know why—perhaps because he had revealed a little about his childhood—but she felt obliged to offer some sort of explanation. 'I used to get teased a lot,' she said quietly.

'Why?'

She stared at him. It was pretty obvious, wasn't it? 'I've always been on the tall side.' She shrugged, keeping her voice light as she added, 'But I'm sure if it hadn't been that it would have been something else. All kids get teased about something.'

He was looking at her too closely and she forced a smile. She was not going to do the hearts and flowers thing, not with Blaise and not now. Thankfully the announcement that they would shortly be landing provided a natural diversion and the piercing blue eyes left her face as the stewardess leant over them, sweetly requesting they fasten their seatbelts. The svelte blonde's gaze lingered just a little too long on Blaise's face but he didn't appear to notice. Kim supposed he was used to it anyway.

It was a smooth landing and the car met them as arranged. Within a short time the driver had taken their luggage to the hotel and they were on their way again. It was clear Blaise knew the driver, Pierre, and she listened to him chatting to the man in fluent French. She had a smattering of the language, enough to get by, but Blaise spoke it like a native. But then anything he did he would do well.

She wondered what it would be like to be made love to by such a man…

'…if you're not too hungry?'

Too late Kim realised Blaise had been talking to her and she hadn't heard a word. She was a normal woman and she had mused about men in a sexual sense in the past, but not in an explicit way and certainly not about someone she knew. Gathering together every scrap of self-control left, she said carefully, 'I'm sorry, I was looking at the scenery.'

'I said I thought I'd like to get the tour of the plant over before we have lunch—that way we've got something to discuss while we eat. If you're not too hungry?'

Blaise's voice had been on the cold side. Kim couldn't blame him. He didn't pay her to daydream. 'No, of course I'm not too hungry,' she said quickly.

'Do you feel all right?' His tone had changed as he peered at her. 'You look a little flushed. Are you unwell?'

'I'm fine.' Her voice came out crisper than she intended. Belatedly, she added lamely, 'But thank you.'

The initial meeting went as well as it could have done in the circumstances. Claude Lemoine was subdued and careful to leave all the talking to Blaise, who made it crystal-clear to Jacques Delbouis exactly what he expected from the takeover.

Kim's earlier feelings of sympathy for Jacques Delbouis were mitigated to some extent when she met the middle-aged Frenchman. He was arrogant, awkward, and on top of everything else clearly fancied himself as God's gift to womankind. When he kissed her hand on meeting her his lips remained on her flesh too long and the look in his eyes when he raised them, along with his oily smile, made Kim want to stamp on his toes.

She took copious notes as the men talked, anxious to miss nothing. After two hours of intensive discussion, she was more than a little relieved when Blaise called a halt for lunch. Her fingers ached, she had the beginnings of a headache and was feeling positively paranoid that she'd missed something vital.

They ate at the Restaurant de l'Etoile, a few streets from the Rue Mouffetard, which Blaise informed her held one of the oldest street markets in Paris. The food was wonderful and Kim thought it was no wonder that French cuisine was considered the finest in the world.

She had expected the meeting to carry on once lunch was over, but instead Blaise told the two men he would see them at the West International premises at six o'clock that evening. 'My lawyers will be there with all the necessary papers. I trust you'll be bringing your legal beagles, Jacques?'

Jacques looked taken aback. 'I was hoping for a few more days to—'

'You've had that and then some.' Blaise's voice had an icy edge to it. 'I'm not prepared to let you procrastinate for another twenty-four hours, let alone several days. Six o'clock or I'm pulling out of the deal and you can look for another buyer.'

For a moment Kim thought the other man was going to argue. He stared at Blaise for a long second, then smiled, shrugging in the expressive way Frenchmen had. *'Les loups ne se mangent pas entre eux,'* he drawled.

'Don't put me to the test.' The icy edge was still there.

'I'll see you and your team at six, Jacques. Claude, you can reach me on my mobile if you need me for anything.'

They left the two men finishing their coffee and, once outside in the pretty cobbled street, Kim said curiously, 'What did he say to you?'

Blaise smiled. It was a cold smile and his eyes were the same when he said, 'He said "wolves don't eat each other". He's wrong, at least where this wolf is concerned. If he's not there tonight with everything in order he can forget it.' His expression changed, becoming wry. 'Aren't you going to make some comment about my hard-heartedness?'

She shook her head. 'I didn't like him.'

'You didn't like him.' Amazingly the sky-blue eyes had a twinkle in them. Kim was so fascinated she couldn't drag her gaze away, even when Blaise took her arm and they began walking out of the side road. He had dismissed the driver when he had dropped them at the restaurant, saying they'd take a taxicab back to the hotel. Obviously the other two men were expected to make their own arrangements. 'I never cease to be amazed at the logic of women,' Blaise murmured. 'You didn't like him and so my…shall we call it firmness,' he asked her, continuing before she could reply, 'is acceptable? What would you have said to my handling of the situation if you *had* liked him?'

'Probably the same.' She knew he was laughing at her but right at this moment she didn't care. She was in Paris on a hot summer's day and something of the city's magic had entered her bloodstream. OK, she was going to be working her socks off getting those notes in order and ready for tonight's meeting but that was par for the course.

'We've a couple of options.' Blaise surveyed her lazily.

'Sorry?'

'We can either go back to the hotel and drop off the papers and then do some sightseeing, or if you're a little tired you could take a nap before we go to the meeting this evening.'

'But I thought you'd want the notes of the meeting by tonight,' Kim said bewilderedly.

They had emerged into the main thoroughfare and Blaise hailed a taxi with consummate ease. 'No. They'll do as a record of what was said and done when we return to England but that's all I wanted. He'll either be there at six tonight or it's all off.'

He helped her into the cab and then got in himself, sitting down beside her, one arm stretched along the back of the seat and his big frame half-turned towards her. 'Well? Sightseeing or rest?'

She didn't have to think twice. 'I've never been to Paris before,' she admitted shyly. 'So sightseeing, please.'

'OK.' He smiled and Kim experienced a sudden tightness in her chest. 'Sightseeing it is.'

It was a heady afternoon. Blaise explained to the taxi driver that Kim had never visited Paris and he wanted her to see as much of the city's lavish gardens, churches, palaces and other places of interest as possible in a few hours. Immediately the driver was a man on a mission. It was clear he was fiercely proud of being a born and bred Parisian, and to show his city off and get paid for it was his idea of heaven.

'*Ah, mademoiselle.*' Careless of the chaotic traffic, he turned in his seat, giving Kim the benefit of a smile revealing blackened teeth. 'You have heard our famous proverb, yes? *Pour être Parisien, il n'est pas nécessaire d'être né à*

*Paris, il suffit d'y renaître.* To be a Parisian one need not be born there, only reborn there.'

Kim smiled nervously, wishing he'd concentrate on driving. 'I'm sure that's right,' she said politely.

'Almost every street has the interest, the—how you say—the memorials, yes?' he continued effusively, thankfully turning to face the windscreen. 'A tree planted by Victor Hugo on the Avenue Raspail, a doorway in Belleville where Edith Piaf was born, a sign—how you say? Ah yes—a mark on the Rue Bellechasse which records the height of our great flood of 1911. It is said whenever France had a moment of glory somewhere in Paris the spectacular arch or statue or column was built. You understand?'

'Yes, yes, I do,' she said hastily, hoping he wasn't going to turn round again to labour the point.

'The Parisian, he has the love of beauty like no other, yes? This is true, *mademoiselle*. I will show you. I, Marcel Piel, will show you.'

Blaise grinned at her. 'You're in the hands of an expert,' he murmured softly. 'Sit back, relax and enjoy.'

The sit back and enjoy bit was easy, relaxing less so with Blaise so close. He wasn't touching any part of her and yet his male warmth seemed to be enveloping her as the cab bumped and wound its way through the city streets and byways. He'd discarded his suit jacket and tie at the beginning of the tour, his open-necked shirt showing the curly black hair of his chest and the muscled strength of his powerful shoulders evident beneath the soft cloth. Kim felt as taut as piano wire.

But the city was enchanting, the countless monuments,

statues, plaques, fountains and squares invariably close to a pavement café or ice-cream vendor. Kim marvelled at the Le Sacré Coeur, which crowned Montmartre, rising like a wedding cake with its elaborate decoration and fancy embellishments, the Palace of Justice, which the driver informed them had been a prison during the Reign of Terror, the Place de la Concorde, where Louis XVI died, swiftly followed by his queen, Marie-Antoinette and hundreds of others, and many other famous landmarks she'd previously only read about in books or seen on the TV.

It was close on four o'clock when they came to the Cimetière du Père-Lachaise, where so many great people were buried. 'We'll stretch our legs for a while,' Blaise told Marcel, turning to Kim as he added, 'You need to walk this place. Many Parisians use it as a park and there's nothing sad or sinister about it; in fact, it's unusually beautiful and tranquil. I brought Lucy here a couple of years ago when we came to Paris for a few days and she spent most of the time playing hide and seek among the tombs with some French children she made friends with.'

Leaving Marcel contentedly puffing on an ancient pipe, they walked into the cemetery, and Kim immediately saw what he meant. It was leafy and green, the sun dappling the weathered tombs and the scent of flowers in the heavy still air. Butterflies and bees busied themselves on the many flowering bushes and a flock of sparrows were twittering in the trees overhead.

They walked side by side through the cobblestone lanes that made up Père-Lachaise, the names on the sleeping tombs reading like a roll call of Napoleon's generals or a dictionary of the great and famous. Balzac, Delacroix,

Colette and Moliere were there, and not only Frenchmen. Among others, Chopin, Oscar Wilde and Sarah Bernhardt were buried there. The whole place was both a reminder of the past and a part of the elusive magic that was Paris.

'Do you think it strange I brought Lucy to a cemetery?' Blaise asked quietly after they had been walking for a few minutes.

Kim looked at him out of the corner of her eye. His face gave nothing away, but then it rarely did. The sun was warm on her head and the perfume from rose bushes sweet in the air as she said carefully, 'No, no really. It's a place of historic interest, isn't it?'

'It is, but that wasn't why I brought my daughter here. She was five years old when her mother was killed and, being a passenger in the car, she unfortunately saw the extent of my wife's injuries. It…wasn't pleasant. She had nightmares for a long time. Her grandmother—' his voice tightened '—is a liability as far as I'm concerned. Around two, two and a half years ago she took it into her head to tell Lucy that there is no heaven and no hell, only what we have here. Now, regardless of her private beliefs, to say that to a child whose comfort was she would see her mother again one day in heaven to my mind was criminal.'

Kim agreed with him. 'How did Lucy react?'

'We had a difficult time of it for a while,' he said grimly. 'But I'd been here before and to me it's special. One gets a feeling of peace. So I brought her here. It was a beautiful summer's day, like today. We talked a little, I reassured her as best I could and then she played with the other children in the sunshine.'

Kim glanced at him. In her mind's eye she saw them, the

big man and small child walking in the scented surroundings among the living and the dead with the sun shining brightly and a blue sky overhead. She swallowed hard over the lump in her throat. 'Did it help?' she asked softly.

Blaise took a deep breath. It was clear he had found talking about the incident difficult. Kim wondered why he had mentioned it. 'Yes, it did.'

'I'm glad.'

'The thing is, Kim, she was younger then. Lately she's got more—I don't know.' He shook his head. 'More in need of a woman to talk to, I guess. Because of what I've told you you can see why I don't encourage her grandmother to be around too much, and although my housekeeper is the backbone of the house she would be the first to say she doesn't understand what makes children tick. But Lucy seemed to take to you. For that reason I wanted you to be aware of how she is before you meet at the weekend.'

Kim stopped in her tracks. If he was hoping Lucy was going to see her as her new best friend he was in for a big disappointment. His daughter had made it quite clear how she viewed her that one time they'd met, and 'favourite auntie' wasn't in the frame. 'Blaise,' she began uncomfortably.

'I'm not asking you to do anything, let me make that clear,' he said before she could continue. 'But if Lucy wanted to talk I thought it only fair to give you a little background. She's been through a lot.'

'Right.' She couldn't say anything but she really wasn't looking forward to the weekend. Perhaps she could have a migraine or something? Even as she thought it she knew she would go. She wanted to see where Blaise lived, see his home. She brushed a stray lock of hair away from her face and tucked it behind her ear. 'I understand that.'

Blaise's gaze followed the action, his face impassive but his voice slightly husky when he said, 'Time's getting on; we'd better get back to the car.'

They didn't speak during the drive back to the hotel but with Marcel as a driver the lack of conversation in the back of the car wasn't noticed. Kim wondered if his jaw ached at night. It should do.

To the taxi driver's delight Blaise asked him to wait while they freshened up and collected the necessary papers, then they were off to the West International building, which was located in a main street close to the Eiffel Tower.

Kim had changed into the cream wool dress for the evening meeting. Teamed with the peep-toe shoes Blaise had bought her and a coffee-coloured, waist-length cashmere cardigan, it was smart but not overly so.

Jacques Delbouis was waiting with his legal team when they arrived at West International. The premises were as large and luxurious as those in London and the same deference was shown to Blaise as he strode through to Claude Lemoine's office, Kim at his side.

The formalities were over very quickly and Jacques didn't appear too distraught at the loss of his company. If anything, Kim thought, he seemed faintly relieved. He smiled his oily smile, shook hands all round and again kissed Kim's hand that fraction too long and then was gone.

'*Fait accompli.*' Claude sank back in his chair as the door closed behind the other man. He emitted a heartfelt sigh.

Blaise smiled. 'He was always going to capitulate. It was just a matter of making things that little bit difficult as far as Jacques was concerned, a matter of pride, perhaps. Let this be a lesson to you, Claude. Always be prepared to walk away from a deal if someone gives you the run-around, no matter how much work you've put into it. And now get yourself home to that long-suffering wife of yours. I'll see you in the morning.'

Pierre was on hand to drive them back to the hotel, Blaise having paid off Marcel on arriving at the building. He must have given the taxi driver a handsome tip if Marcel's extravagant declarations of undying loyalty were anything to go by.

As they walked into the hotel foyer, Blaise glanced at his Rolex. 'Ten to seven and I've reserved a table for dinner for eight,' he said quietly. 'Shall we say half-past seven in the cocktail bar?'

She nodded breathlessly as they stepped into the lift and once on their floor disappeared quickly into her room, which was some distance from Blaise's. It was a beautiful room. The hotel was beautiful. *Life* was beautiful around Blaise, she thought a trifle hysterically. Smooth and fluid without any hiccups.

And yet not really. She stood in the large, luxurious room, her mind racing. His wealth and influence could buy most things but his marriage had failed and he had a ten-year-old daughter who wasn't happy by the sound of it. And he was worried about her. She wondered if he had any idea what a poignant combination the image of hard, tough tycoon and tender father was. Deadly, in fact.

'You're just his personal assistant,' she reminded herself sternly. And talking to yourself was the first sign of madness.

She didn't change before she went down to the cocktail

bar but she put her hair up in a more sophisticated style than she normally wore for the office, and applied a little extra make-up to her eyes.

At exactly half-past seven she went downstairs. Blaise was already seated in the cocktail bar with a drink in front of him, and for a moment she stood and surveyed him, aware he couldn't see her behind the huge fern at the entrance. He was sitting in brooding silence despite the efforts of two young women at a nearby table trying to catch his eye. His natural physical presence and relaxed sexuality were more apparent in the room of smiling, chatting people, and the words Jacques Delbouis had spoken came back to her. Blaise looked like a wolf among a flock of amiable sheep, she thought shakily, at present content to sit and watch them at play but with the leashed power to change stance in an instant. That undefinable dangerous quality he had was part of his attraction but she'd never fully grasped it before.

As she walked over to him she saw the two women give her the once-over and she knew what they were thinking. How come someone like her is with him? Her chin lifting, she returned Blaise's smile, sitting down in the seat he indicated as he stood up, saying, 'What can I get you to drink?'

'What are you having?'

'This? A champagne cocktail. The barman here does them particularly well. Some places just add brandy to the champagne and try and pass it off as a cocktail, but Henri does it properly.'

'Which is?'

Blaise bent closer, one hand on the back of her chair, and every nerve in Kim's body tightened. 'He moistens a white sugar cube with two dashes of Angostura bitters and places it in a champagne flute. Then he adds the brandy and gently pours in an excellent dry champagne. Come and watch if you like.'

'Can I?'

'Of course—that's half the fun in these places and Henri likes nothing more than an audience.'

Henri proved to be a genial soul with gentle eyes and a wide smile. And the cocktail was delicious. So delicious Kim had another one when Blaise asked her. At eight o'clock when they walked through to the restaurant she told herself no more alcohol until she had eaten something, although she wasn't sure if it was the cocktails or Blaise's company that was making her feel giddy and excited.

The restaurant was all glittering crystal and snow-white tablecloths and waiters gliding about as though they were on rollers. They were shown to a table for two in a small alcove close to where the pianist was quietly playing.

'This is lovely.' Kim turned bright eyes to Blaise as the waiter disappeared after presenting them both with an embossed menu. 'Do you always stay here when you come to Paris?'

He nodded. 'It suits me.'

Kim studied his face, taking in his blue eyes, the chiselled face structure, the strong jaw. If Blaise was attractive in working mode, he was ten times more lethal as a dinner companion. For the last half an hour he had set himself out to entertain her, his wit sharp and his conversation amusing and light, just like that other time she'd had dinner with him.

Did he find her boring? It wasn't a new thought. From the first day of working for Blaise she had been impressed by his intimidating intelligence and keen, dry humour. And the women he usually dated were beautiful, independent and strong, career women on the whole, she understood, but often with an edge that made them successful in their field.

She looked down at the menu. Thankfully it was in English as well as French and consisted of five courses with a wide selection in each.

Having mentally decided what she wanted, she glanced up again to find Blaise's eyes on her face. 'You look very lovely tonight, Kim,' he murmured in a rather self-derisory tone.

She stared at him, unable to determine the reason for the look on his face or the tenor of his voice. 'Thank you,' she said, a trifle uncertainly.

The waiter came across at that moment and took their order after pouring them a glass of the wine Blaise had ordered earlier. Nerves prompted Kim to take a sip. It was luscious, packed with ripe honeyed melon, lime and fig flavours. Kim had requested white after the champagne, feeling if she stuck with the same colour it might be less potent, but, having tasted the wine, she doubted it. She was no wine connoisseur like Blaise but she recognised an expensive one when she tasted it.

Blaise had tasted a small sample when the waiter had poured the wine; now he said, 'Is it to your liking?'

'It's wonderful.' She took another sip and then put her glass down, telling herself she needed at least two courses under her belt before she had any more. 'You obviously know a lot about wine.'

'I've discovered what I like over the years, that's all, or perhaps more importantly what I don't like,' he said, a smile curving his lips. 'Trial and error, like all of life.'

Kim nodded.

'Has there been much trial and error in your life, Kim?' he asked softly.

Her eyes widened for a moment. 'Some,' she said warily.

When she didn't elaborate the blue eyes narrowed. 'Involving a man?'

This wasn't like Blaise. She had discovered he rarely asked personal questions unless they were directly related to the job in hand. Quietly, she said, 'Yes, involving a man, but it was some time ago.'

'What's some time ago?' And then he raised his hand, saying, 'I'm sorry, you don't have to answer that.'

'It's all right.' Although it wasn't. She didn't want to talk about David and especially not to Blaise, but after what he'd confided about Lucy that afternoon she felt obliged to say more. 'Some time ago is a couple of years and involved a broken engagement.'

'You were going to get *married*?'

His tone needled her. 'You find that so surprising?'

He picked up his wine glass as he considered. 'Yes, I do,' he said slowly. 'I haven't known you long but you strike me as the sort of woman who would have to be sure it was going to work out before you took such a big step.'

Faintly mollified, Kim found the courage to say, 'It wasn't me who broke off the engagement.'

After a long moment spent searching her face, he said softly, 'What a fool he must have been.'

She hadn't expected that. Blinking, she shrugged. 'Far better than going through with it, though.'

'Is it too painful to talk about?'

'Do you mean, am I over him?' she said quietly, careful

to keep her voice neutral despite the unhappy memories his questions had evoked. 'Completely. I have been for a long while, but such an experience makes one…distrustful, I suppose.'

'Of men?'

'In a nutshell.' She forced a smile. 'Although I do realise you aren't all tarred with the same brush.'

'Thank you,' he said drily. He settled back in his chair, taking another sip of his drink before he said, 'No doubt the ever-efficient grapevine has informed you of my own venture into togetherness and the dire results?'

It was said lightly, mockingly, but somehow Kim knew that wasn't how he was feeling inside. 'I know you were married and divorced, if that's what you mean.'

'Discreet and tactful to the last.'

Kim's eyes went a shade darker. What did he expect her to say?

'I'm sorry.' Blaise shook his head at his crassness. 'It's just that there are times when I feel I live my life in a goldfish bowl. What they don't know, they make up. Still, I'd be the first to admit it comes with the territory.'

'That doesn't make it right or fair,' she said softly, her heart beating so hard she was sure he must see it. She hadn't expected the evening to take this direction.

'True.' He smiled but it didn't reach the piercingly blue eyes. 'Still, the whole experience taught me one thing that has stood me in good stead.'

Kim raised her eyebrows. 'Oh?'

'That love is just a four-letter word that means less than the paper it's written on.'

His words were like a dash of cold water, even as she

asked herself why. She'd known he was hard and cynical, hadn't she?

'But I guess I'm preaching to the converted,' he said quietly, 'after what you've gone through.'

'If you're asking whether I believe in love and marriage and for ever, then yes, I do. With the right person, of course. And David clearly wasn't, for me. Whether I'll come across the right one I don't know, but I'd be careful not to be taken for a ride again.'

'How?'

'What?'

'How can you be sure you won't meet another David? You must have thought you loved him and he you but it didn't work out. How can you be sure history won't repeat itself?'

There was something in his voice, an intensity, that took her by surprise. Shifting in her seat, a small, uneasy movement, she wondered why conversations with Blaise tended to resemble minefields. 'I don't suppose I can,' she conceded after a moment or two. 'Nothing in life is certain. We could walk out of here and get knocked down by a bus tomorrow or the plane could crash on the way home, anything.'

'Great,' he muttered laconically.

'But that doesn't mean we should sit here for ever. After—after David I had to change direction, decide what to do with the rest of my life because the future I thought was all mapped out had changed with one conversation. I realised then I might never meet anyone else, and frankly I'm not altogether sure if I want to, but if it happened I hope I'd be brave enough to take that gamble and try again.'

'So you do admit it would be a gamble?'

'To some extent. But I am older and wiser and I think I wouldn't make some of the mistakes I made then. I wouldn't be so blindly trusting for one thing, however besotted I was.'

A silence descended in which the conversation and occasional laughter from the other tables and the pianist's soft melody seemed somehow muted. Blaise wasn't looking at her now, his gaze as brooding and dark as it had been in the cocktail bar before he had seen her. 'There are some gambles where the odds are far too high to make it worthwhile,' he said flatly after a full minute had screamed by, the muscle that jumped in his jaw belying the expressionless tone.

Kim's pulse gave a funny leap. 'I suppose that's for every man and woman to decide for themselves.' Her voice was calm and composed, she noted with satisfaction.

'Possibly, but when a third person could be affected I think you'd agree it's a whole new ball game.'

Kim looked him full in the face as he glanced her way. 'You mean someone like Lucy, for example?' she said bravely, deciding there'd been enough cloak-and-dagger. Was he seeing someone at the moment he was particularly interested in? she wondered. Someone he wasn't sure Lucy would take to?

'Hypothetically, yes.' His voice was cold, colourless. 'Children don't ask to be born into a broken family. Hell, they don't ask to be born at all.' He stopped abruptly and Kim watched him gain the control that had momentarily slipped. He inhaled deeply but inaudibly, letting his breath out before he said, 'I've seen one or two situations where people have married for the third or fourth time and there are kids from each marriage. Some of those kids can barely work out who's who.'

'That's extreme, though, and hardly the norm,' she said quietly.

'Yes, I'll give you that.' His eyes were distracted; he was gazing inward to a memory she couldn't share. 'But I don't suppose any of them planned it that way; it just got so it was impossible to live with the person they'd married.'

'Lots of people live all their lives with one person and are very happy,' she said in the same quiet tone, 'but they don't make the news in the same way as those who break up. There's that to consider.'

He glanced at her earnest face. Their eyes held for a long moment and then his features relaxed, although a remnant of something dark remained. He glanced over her shoulder. 'Here's our first course,' he said lightly, as though they had been discussing nothing more controversial than the weather. *'Bon appétit.'*

## CHAPTER SEVEN

FOR the rest of the evening Blaise continued the role of amusing dinner companion and he did it so successfully that Kim didn't begin to relive their conversation from before the meal until she was back in her room. Then she found she couldn't think about anything else and she certainly couldn't sleep.

At two in the morning she called Room Service for a mug of hot chocolate and a plate of biscuits. They provided the comfort factor but she was still no nearer dozing off at three o'clock when she settled down in bed again. Of all the men in the world she could have worked for, she had to get stuck with the most complicated, enigmatic and possibly the most attractive one, she thought wryly. Not that that was a problem, it wasn't—she could cope perfectly well, she told herself firmly. But somehow over the last weeks she felt she had been drawn into Blaise's life in a way she never had with her previous employers.

Twisting onto her side, she gazed across the beautiful gold and cream room, which was faintly lit by one lamp on the long desk in a corner.

And it should be just the opposite, that was the puzzling

thing. Blaise was more ruthless and detached than anyone else she'd met, an almost completely autonomous being, except for his daughter, of course. So how come she felt so disturbed and restless tonight just because of their conversation earlier?

*Because you've fallen in love with him.*

Kim sat sharply upright as the thought hit. She had not, of course she hadn't. She *was* sexually attracted to him, she admitted, but then most women would be. He had that undefinable magnetism that had nothing to do with good looks or wealth but all to do with something in the man himself. But lust wasn't love.

'It isn't.' She spoke out loud, needing to hear the sound of herself saying it. Just because she was constantly assailed by an inconvenient ache of desire when she was with Blaise—and even when she wasn't, actually, she acknowledged ruefully—it did not mean she loved him. It would be emotional suicide to fall in love with him, and she had had more than enough devastation in that area to last her a lifetime.

When—*if*—she gave her heart to someone, it would have to be a man she could rely on, and most definitely he would have to be crazy about her before she even considered him in that way. Nothing else would do. That was the whole reason she'd done such a lot of heart-searching and decided to follow the career route, because she knew she might have to live her life without marriage, children…

'I do not love him,' she stated firmly, and then groaned. It didn't make it any less a lie by saying it.

She was an idiot. A prize-winning, 24-carat idiot. She wrapped her arms round her knees, swaying to and fro as her face burnt and she fought back hot tears.

What could she do? Leave him? Leave the job, leave West International altogether?

Immediately everything in her repudiated the idea. She couldn't. It wasn't even a logical answer, she assured herself quickly. Emotionally it wouldn't solve anything because she would still love him whether she went or stayed, and to walk out on such a terrific job without a valid reason—and that was the way Blaise would look at it because she couldn't tell him the truth, so it would have to be some weak excuse—would scupper her career for sure. No, she'd have to stay and get over it. She swallowed hard.

This was only a problem if she made it one. That was what she had to remember. Millions of people fell in love and had to accept it could never be returned; it wasn't such a big deal. She'd get over it. That was what folk did, wasn't it?

Kim repeated this in a hundred different ways over the next couple of hours, and at half-past five gave up all thoughts of sleep and had a long, warm shower, washing her hair and creaming and moisturising all over. She might have made the worst mistake of her life by falling in love with the most unsuitable man in England, if not the world, but that still didn't mean she couldn't look her best.

At six-thirty she made her way downstairs for an early breakfast, not because she was particularly hungry, she wasn't, not after the chocolate and biscuits, but because sitting alone in her room just thinking was not an option.

When she walked into the restaurant Blaise wasn't on her mind for the first time in hours but she was wondering what the procedure for breakfast was. Consequently, after telling the waitress it was breakfast for one she followed her straight past the big dark man sitting in solitary splendour at a table for two.

'Kim?' Blaise's smoky voice halted her in her tracks. 'What are you doing down so early?'

Flushing hotly, she tried to gather herself. 'I—I couldn't sleep,' she stammered. 'Strange bed.'

He nodded. 'I couldn't sleep either.'

He looked tired. Why was it, Kim asked herself, that men could look ten times more sexy when they were tired and women only looked haggard? There was something wrong there. Unutterably glad she had taken the time to put some make-up on and brush her newly conditioned and shining hair into sleek obedience, Kim slid into the seat he gestured to.

'I've ordered coffee but if you prefer tea...?' he said quietly.

'Yes, please.' She smiled at the waitress, who was standing to one side watching them.

Once she had disappeared, Blaise smiled the lazy smile he did so well. 'So this is what you look like first thing in the morning. I'm impressed.'

Returning the smile with some effort, Kim felt herself grow warm. 'Not really,' she said carefully. 'Like I said, I couldn't sleep, so it's not a true representation.'

'I don't believe that.' His tone was light but something had changed in his eyes, subtly, almost imperceptibly. 'You have a natural beauty that doesn't need enhancing with cosmetics and fancy hairdos. I know women who strive for hours for the natural look and fail miserably.'

Women he had wined and dined and bedded, no doubt. Deep inside her she felt a sinking sensation but it didn't show in her voice when she said brightly, 'How do you know I haven't been up all night trying to look fresh and sparkling?'

'Have you?'

'Well, I couldn't sleep, like I said, but no, fresh and sparkling wasn't high on my agenda. Just sleep.'

The waitress returned with their tea and coffee, and after they had helped themselves to orange juice and croissants from the extensive buffet, which seemed to hold every breakfast combination known to man, they began a leisurely meal.

The restaurant filled up in the hour they sat there but Kim wasn't really conscious of the other diners, only Blaise. Her new awareness of her feelings was both frightening and strangely fascinating. She found herself watching every slight movement he made, every turn of his head, every expression that passed over the hard, attractive face.

When they left the restaurant and walked to the lift to return to their respective rooms, his touch on her elbow made her flesh burn through the thin blouse she was wearing. It was extreme and probably wildly dramatic, she told herself as the lift took them smoothly upwards, but she felt as though she had never been truly alive until she met Blaise. There was a part of her which had been sleeping, a part David hadn't even begun to impinge on. Which made it all the more imperative Blaise never guessed how she felt. She had felt the humiliation and embarrassment she'd gone through when David called off the wedding was the worst thing that could happen to her; she'd been wrong. Meeting Blaise had confirmed that. It would be ten times, a hundred times more crushing for

Blaise to tell her thanks but no thanks, as she would fully expect him to do if he caught a hint of her feelings. And that would be the end of the job too.

The willpower that had carried her through the mortifying aftermath of her broken engagement with her head held high and a smile stitched on her face kept her cool and collected on the way back to England, despite the turmoil within.

They went straight to the office after landing at Heathrow and the rest of the day was so busy it left no room for agonising. The remainder of the week proved to be the same. And in the evenings she had long telephone conversations with a few friends she hadn't caught up with in latter weeks, had a mini spring clean of the flat and generally kept herself so busy she didn't have time for useless contemplation.

On Saturday morning Kim woke very early. Padding to the window, she drew back the curtains and looked out on to a soft summer morning that promised a glorious hot day.

She hadn't slept well, mainly due to the fact that the evening before, shortly after she had got home, Blaise had phoned. 'We didn't arrange about the weekend,' he'd started off, his tone making it clear he considered it an oversight on her part not to have reminded him. As she had determined after Paris not to mention Lucy's birthday celebrations and just wait and see if he did, she remained silent, although her heart had geared up a few beats. The bright pink invitation had been pretty general, merely stating lunch would be a barbeque round the pool and could everyone bring their swimming costumes, and there'd be dancing to a band later in the evening. Blaise lived in Harrow, and so in view of the journey involved and his casual attitude when he had given her the invitation, and, not least, the realisation that he meant more to her than just her boss, Kim had decided not to go unless he specifically asked her.

'Kim?' he had said a trifle irritably. 'Did you hear what I said? You hadn't forgotten it was Lucy's birthday this weekend?'

Of course she hadn't forgotten! She had spent the last two lunchtimes scouring the shops for a present for a child who had everything, telling herself if she didn't go to the party she would give the gift to Blaise on Monday morning with the excuse something had come up to prevent her attending. She'd rapidly discarded the idea of clothes; Lucy had been so tiny she wouldn't know what size to buy her and clothes were such a personal thing anyway.

Eventually she had found something she thought would do in a tiny little shop which specialised in accessories for females from the age of two to a hundred and two! The little watch was crafted from wood, the face being set into a flower shape and the bracelet comprising of small wooden beads. It was simple, unusual and funky, and the shopkeeper had assured her that her own twelve-year-old daughter had several in different colours. Not knowing Lucy's taste, Kim kept her choice to a natural wood rather than one of the painted ones.

Now she answered Blaise carefully, saying, 'No, I hadn't forgotten.'

'We need to arrange a time for me to pick you up.'

She had stared at the receiver for a moment before saying, 'I don't expect you to do that; I can make my own way there.'

'Nonsense.' It had been brisk; he was clearly tiring of the conversation. 'Most folk are arriving around one o'clock, so I'll pick you up about half-past eleven—that'll give us plenty of time even on a Saturday morning. Be ready, won't you?'

She'd stammered some sort of a reply and in typical Blaise fashion that had been the end of the conversation. She had sat staring at the telephone for a full minute before jumping up and going into a frenzy of clothes sorting.

Kim turned from the window now, going over to the wardrobe and opening it. At one end she'd hung the clothes she intended to pack for the day. Fortunately, due to a girly holiday with three friends the year before, she had a fabulous coffee-coloured bikini and sarong which she knew showed off her full-breasted, narrow-waisted figure to full advantage. However, what had seemed like a good idea when she'd been on holiday with three extrovert girlfriends didn't seem like quite such a good idea in the cold light of a British barbeque round the pool. It wasn't that the bikini wasn't expensive or good enough—it had cost her a small fortune at the time—it was more the thought of appearing in front of Blaise so scarcely clad that was panicking her.

But she could keep the sarong on all the time if she wanted, she comforted herself in the next moment. In fact, she didn't have to change into swimwear at all if she didn't want to; there was bound to be some people who didn't. And although the cut of the half-cup bra of the bikini gave her full breasts an extra voluptuousness, it was no more than the average cocktail dress would do. It wasn't actually indecent or anything.

Her eyes moved to the dress she'd chosen for the evening. It was the same one she had taken to Paris but never worn. It was another buy for the holiday the year before and she had followed her instincts when she'd purchased it, knowing that her friends—all under five-foot-seven—would have sexy little empire-line dresses with coquettishly styled flounces and ties and flirty frills. But she wasn't cute and slender. And so she had embraced the draped silk-jersey dress with its plunging neckline when she'd come across it, knowing both the pale gold colour and the seductive cut were what was needed to hold her own with them. The metallic Cleopatra-style necklace and bracelet she'd bought at the same time set the dress off to perfection, and she needed to feel good today. She might be the Cinderella of the occasion, and she still didn't know how Lucy was going to be with her, but if she looked her best she could take whatever came in her stride. Hopefully.

She forced down a breakfast she had no inclination for, nerves playing havoc with her normal healthy appetite, and was ready long before eleven-thirty. Blaise came precisely on time and as soon as she heard the doorbell ring her heart jumped into her mouth. The flats had an intercom system for security and she pressed the button with shaky fingers, her voice something of a squeak when she croaked, 'Hello?'

'Kim? It's me, Blaise.'

Swallowing hard against her wildly hammering heart, she managed to say fairly steadily 'I'm just coming' as she pressed the switch to release the door to the house.

She grabbed her overnight bag and opened her own front door but he was already standing in the large hall, big and dark against the cream-painted walls. 'Hi.' It was soft and smoky and his eyes ran over her as she smiled nervously. 'You look as fresh as a summer's day.'

Kim found she didn't know how to take that. Did he mean fresh as in scrubbed schoolmarm or fresh as in gorgeous? She thought the white and silver-grey flowered sleeveless dress struck just the right casual but smart note for a birthday celebration but maybe the wow factor was missing. Not that she could wow Blaise anyway, she acknowledged in the next moment.

'So you have a ground-floor flat? Any garden?' he asked lazily.

She hadn't wanted to ask him in. That was why she had been ready so early. Her flat was *her* space, her private sanctuary. She hadn't wanted to picture Blaise in it somehow. Politeness demanded differently however. 'No, just a small patio area. Would you like to see?'

He nodded, walking across to her. He was dressed in a short-sleeved white linen shirt, open at the neck, and black denim jeans, tight across the hips. Kim thought he should have a notice attached to him—'Too hot to handle.'

He followed her into the flat and she was vitally conscious of his brand of flagrant masculinity as she turned in the sitting room, saying, 'The patio doors lead onto my tiny garden but it's more than the other folk get, so I'm not complaining.'

She was wearing flat pumps and he seemed to tower over her as she threw open the French doors after pulling aside the muslin drapes. He stood alongside her, looking over her tiny square of paved garden, which was a riot of colour with flowering tubs and sweet-smelling pots of herbs and flowers. Her small bistro table and two chairs stood in the middle of the ensemble, the black wrought-iron a contrast to the colour and brightness surrounding them.

'This is nice.' His voice was warm, appreciative. 'It makes me want to sit and relax.'

'It's a sun trap,' she said quietly, 'and perfect for mild spring and autumn days as well as summer. I often sit and read out here.'

He smiled. 'Curled up like a small, contented cat. I can picture it.'

Small? But then, she supposed anyone was small when compared to his great height. 'It's not a window seat in a mansion,' she corrected firmly, trying not to concentrate on what his words had engendered. It felt so good to be viewed as something so sensual and serene as a purring feline. 'I dare anyone to try and curl up on one of these seats.'

'A moving symphony of colour,' he said softly.

'I beg your pardon?'

'Your hair. I've been trying to decide what colour it is but then I realised it would be like trying to catch sunbeams and define them.' He lifted a large hand and let a lock of her hair feather through his fingers. 'Beautiful...'

She stood as still as stone, not daring to move. He had surprised her, more than surprised her, and she didn't know how to react. Belatedly she realised she needed to say something light and witty, as one of his sophisticated and worldy-wise women would have done, but for the life of her nothing came to mind. She took refuge in the mundane, stepping forward and closing the floor-length windows as she said briskly, 'We need to go if you are going to be back in time to welcome your guests.'

His expression changed to a quizzical ruffle. 'You're off

duty today, Kim. Relax. Just enjoy yourself like anyone else. And they're Lucy's guests, not mine. She chose who'd attend.'

In other words if it had been left to him she wouldn't have been invited. Hiding the spasm of pain, she said evenly, 'Well, if nothing else you ought to be at her side helping her, surely?'

He nodded. 'You're right. As always.' He turned away from her and she felt bereft for a moment. 'Come on, then, bossy.' Now his tone was almost playful. 'But remember what I said. You are Kim Abbott, party-goer, today. Not Kim Abbott, efficient personal assistant. OK?'

'OK.'

Once Kim had folded herself into the Ferrari she felt a wave of heat pass through her body as Blaise slid in beside her. His nearness made her all fingers and thumbs as she fumbled with the safety belt and after a second he clicked his tongue, leaning over her in his usual impatient way and fastening it for her.

His aftershave wafted faintly on the air, tantalising her senses, its subtle overtones of lime and oak and something purely Blaise tightening her lower stomach. It was going to be a long journey, Kim told herself wryly.

# CHAPTER EIGHT

THE drive from Kim's flat in Guildford to Harrow was accomplished in well under an hour, despite the Saturday chaos which always caused delays. Blaise was a relaxed and skilful driver, weaving in and out of the traffic with consummate ease and controlling the powerful car with little effort.

They chatted about this and that on the way there and Kim was pleased with the way she kept up her end of the conversation, considering how she was feeling inside. Blaise was right, she *did* have to chill a little, she told herself sternly. She was attending a birthday party and no doubt there would be plenty of Blaise's friends and acquaintances there, as well as Lucy's circle. They would be sophisticated, wealthy and all the women would probably be elegant lovelies, knowing her luck, but that didn't matter. As long as she could get through the day without disgracing herself she'd never see the majority of them again for the rest of her life.

Kim had known Blaise's house wouldn't be a two-up, two-down terrace, but when the Ferrari eventually turned through wide-open gates onto a long gravel driveway she wasn't prepared for the beautiful 18th-century manor house that confronted her. It was long and three-storeyed, small mullioned windows peeping out from under the eaves and a roof of weathered pale tiles complementing the mellow stone beneath. Fat old plane tress stood either side of the house, providing dappled shade, and ivy and wisteria lent more colour to the whole.

Peaceful wasn't a word she would have associated with Blaise, but that was what the house looked. Peaceful and tranquil and curiously unpretentious, considering its size.

'It's beautiful.' As they stopped in front of the house she turned to Blaise. 'Perfect for bringing up a child.'

'I think so. After the divorce I bought an apartment a few blocks from the office and my wife and Lucy stayed in the house we had in Richmond, but once the accident happened everything changed. I wanted to get Lucy into a proper home.'

It seemed a strange thing to say. 'Wasn't the house in Richmond a proper home?'

'It was a typical town house, I guess. No garden but the last word in luxury. Miranda saw it just before we got married and nothing else would do.' He shrugged. 'Not suitable for a family in my opinion.'

It was the first time he had spoken his wife's name and ridiculously it hurt. Which was completely illogical. Kim nodded. 'This is much better,' she said firmly.

The stern lips twisted in an amused smile. 'I'm glad you approve. Here the garden is big enough for Lucy to have some space. The pool is at the back of the house in an extension the previous owners had built, and she's a good swimmer.'

He opened his door as he finished speaking, walking round the bonnet and then helping her out of the Ferrari and taking her bag. 'I hope you don't mind dogs,' he said as they walked up the steps to the front door. 'We have two Labradors and a cocker spaniel, but they would lick you to death if anything.'

She smiled. 'I love dogs.' Again she couldn't have said she'd put Blaise down as a pet owner, but this was a whole new side to him she was seeing.

'I think children should be brought up with animals if at all possible,' he said, opening the front door and ushering her into a vast sunlit hall. 'It gives them a better perspective on life. Do you know what I mean?'

Actually, she did. But animals were ties and again she hadn't seen Blaise putting his hand up for that.

'What?' She hadn't been aware he was watching her so closely but now she became aware his eyes were tight on her face as she brought her gaze from the paintings on the white walls. 'What are you thinking?'

Kim blinked, but with the piercingly blue eyes trained on her she found her thought process had frozen. Feeling it would be worse to prevaricate than tell the truth, she said weakly, 'I hadn't expected you to be the sort of man who would have pets but I suppose you wanted them for Lucy.'

'That's what you suppose, is it?' His voice was mild but she could tell he hadn't liked her confession. 'Actually I had the two Labradors for myself; I like Labs. The cocker spaniel is Lucy's.'

He didn't have time to say anything more before a door to their right opened and all three dogs and Lucy streamed into the hall. Fussing the dogs, who immediately presented themselves in a well-behaved circle round her legs, got Kim over the awkward first few minutes with Lucy, but then a stout, middle-aged woman appeared whom Blaise introduced as Mrs Maclean, the housekeeper. After a couple of pleasantries Mrs Maclean shooed the dogs away down the hall into what Kim assumed was the kitchen, saying over her shoulder, 'Let's at least get everyone here without these three underfoot. I'll keep them in the kitchen with me for the time being.' She paused at the door once the dogs were in the kitchen, turning to say, 'Everything's ready down by the pool, by the way, but I'm having nothing to do with the barbeque, Mr West.' Her gaze switching to Kim, she added, 'Why folk want to eat burnt offerings in the open air with the flies and goodness knows what, I really don't know. Not when they can have a perfectly good meal indoors which has the advantage of being cooked properly.'

With that she sniffed loudly and entered the kitchen, shutting the door very firmly behind her.

'You might have gathered Mrs Maclean is not a devotee of outdoor eating and especially barbeques,' Blaise said drily as Kim looked at him in astonishment. She could hardly believe he had allowed his housekeeper to talk to him in such a fashion but Lucy was giggling at his side.

'Mac doesn't like pierced ears, short skirts, dyed hair, painted nails and she'd die if me or Dad got a tattoo,' the girl confided. 'She's *so* old-fashioned.'

'But very good to us, young lady, and don't you forget it.' Blaise's voice was mild but it was a warning none the less.

Lucy grimaced. 'But *all* the girls at school have got pierced ears.' She glanced at Kim's silver hoops. 'How old were you when you had yours done?'

Feeling she was in something of a minefield, Kim cast

an apologetic glance at Blaise as she answered truthfully, 'I had them pierced for my tenth birthday.'

'There, you see?' Lucy pressed small fists on non-existent hips. 'I'm the only girl in the whole school, probably the whole *world*, who hasn't had hers done.'

'We're not having this conversation again and not *now*.' The mildness had gone from Blaise's tone. 'Kim is your guest and you're supposed to be looking after her, not embarrassing her.'

Kim expected a mini-explosion after the opinion she'd formed of Blaise's daughter after the incident in the hospital car park. Instead Lucy looked straight at her. 'Sorry,' she said as though she meant it. 'Would you like me to show you around while Dad answers his calls?' Turning to her father, she added, 'There have been three since you've been gone. Mac was doing the desserts for tonight so I said I'd man the phone. I've written them down on the pad in your study but one was urgent. From…?' the small, straight nose wrinkled '…Robert Turner of Turner Fabrics.'

'Hell, what now?' Blaise glanced at Kim. 'Would you mind?'

'I'd love Lucy to show me round,' Kim lied cheerfully, still not sure where the girl was coming from.

Within a minute or two she'd had to revise her opinion of Blaise's daughter though. Lucy suggested they go to her room first, where she said Kim could leave her things and then change later if she wanted to swim, and once they had climbed the stairs to the first floor and entered an enormous pink and white bedroom, Lucy said without any preamble, 'Thanks for not saying anything to Dad.'

'About what?' Kim was still wary.

'About me being rude to you the other day. I—I was in a temper, I suppose. Mac and Dad still treat me like a baby. I mean, as if I couldn't wait in Dad's car for a while by myself!'

Feeling honesty was the best option, Kim said gently, 'I don't think it was that. I think he was worried you might be a bit upset with it being a hospital, that's all.'

'I told him I wouldn't.'

'But he's your dad and he loves you. My dad's still the same with me and I'm twenty-five.'

Lucy looked at her for a long moment. 'Really?'

'Really.' Deciding enough had been said, Kim glanced round the room. It was the perfect haven for a young girl, from the twin beds—for when Lucy had a friend to sleep over—complete with pink and white cushions and white lace covers, to the ankle-deep white carpet. The walls were painted white but the ceiling was a mural of snowy-white clouds, birds and butterflies against a blue sky. Shelves holding cuddly toys and dolls and books took up the whole of one wall, and a long, low child-size computer table and desk and chair another, with all the latest equipment and games. The most enormous doll's house stood in one corner, which Kim realised was a mini replica of Blaise's house. The room also held a large walk-in wardrobe and *en suite*. Everything a little girl could want, Kim thought with a stab of pity, but the most important thing: a mother.

By the time Lucy had shown her over most of the house the two of them were talking quite naturally. Blaise joined them just as Lucy was about to take her through to the swimming pool and garden, his eyes taking in their relaxed manner, with something in his expression Kim couldn't read.

The swimming pool, like the rest of the house, was

stunning, its retractable roof open to the sunshine and its huge glass doors leading onto a stone-flagged terrace, bordered with earthenware pots and scattered with outdoor wicker furniture, beyond which the rest of the garden stretched. A bar stood to one side of the pool and was well-stocked, bowls of nuts and olives on its granite counter.

'Oh, I nearly forgot.' Kim fished Lucy's present and card out of her handbag. 'Happy birthday.'

Lucy thanked her politely but then her face lit up when she opened the small box. 'This is brilliant, Kim; Fiona Harcastle's got one like this…they're so cool,' she said delightedly as she took off a slim gold wristwatch and slipped Kim's over her small wrist.

'I don't think it's pool-proof,' Kim warned smilingly.

'It's great; I'm just going to show Mac.'

So saying, she skipped off and Blaise said, 'Glass of wine before lunch?' as he waved his hand at one of the cushioned chairs on the terrace.

'You must have loads to do,' Kim said quickly. 'Don't worry about me.'

'I'm not worried.' His eyes were narrowed against the sun, his black hair and tanned skin all the darker against the white of his shirt. 'And there's nothing to do. If this follows other such days people will arrive in dribs and drabs and want to swim for a bit before we eat. Everyone helps themselves to drinks and so on; it's very casual.'

'Right.' She wished she could be. 'Then a glass of wine would be lovely, thank you.'

As she sat in the chair he'd indicated Blaise fetched a bottle and two glasses. Sitting down beside her, he poured them both some wine and handed Kim a glass. 'Thanks.'

She sipped the liquid, pleased to find it was cool and citrussy, tart on her tongue.

She looked up to find his gaze lingering on the silky-smooth curtain of her hair. As blue eyes met dark brown, Blaise cleared his throat. 'I'm glad you could come today, Kim.'

She stared at him. The tone was wrong. He didn't sound glad at all. 'When Lucy wanted to invite you I thought it might be a good way of acquainting you with my home circumstances, which it's important for a PA to be aware of.'

Something had changed in the last little while. He wasn't the same as he'd been earlier that morning. She searched her mind for where she'd gone wrong.

'Of course, some women might get the wrong idea about such an invitation but I know you're far too sensible to imagine…'

For the first time it dawned on her where he was coming from. He was warning her off, she thought incredulously. He was actually warning her off from having any ideas about him.

Kim's temper was of the slow-boil variety, but once the flame was lit it rarely went out before a hundred degrees centigrade.

'To imagine?' she repeated, saccharine-sweet, her eyebrows raised as she told herself to pay him in his own coin.

Blaise shrugged. 'I don't believe in mixing work and pleasure.'

'I should hope not.' Her level tone was more chilling than blatant anger. 'Sexual harassment is an ugly thing.'

Blaise's facial muscles tightened. 'I wasn't talking about sexual or physical intimidation exactly.'

'No? Then what *exactly* did you mean?' She purposely kept her voice cool even though inwardly she was calling him names she hadn't even been aware were in her psyche and which would cause her mother to faint on the spot. The only thing which kept her from throwing her wine in his face and insisting he get her a taxi was that the swine was looking uncomfortable—that and the fact that she loved him.

'It doesn't matter.'

Oh, yes, it did. 'OK.' The smile was the best bit of acting she had ever done and she took a sip of wine as though their conversation hadn't been at all important.

He was looking nonplussed, as well he might, Kim thought furiously. He clearly wasn't sure if she had caught on to what he was saying. Which, if you thought about it, was just as insulting as telling her to keep her hands off him.

Their gazes caught and held, and whether something in her eyes revealed her anger she didn't know, but the next moment his expression changed and he leant forward, saying, 'Kim, I didn't mean…' He shook his head. 'It's just that I don't get involved any more. The women I date know the score—'

'Why are you telling me this, Blaise?' Kim interrupted tightly. That was the best thing about having a temper, she'd always found; the years of teasing and taunting she'd endured in her early teens had taught her that, controlled properly, rage could put iron in her backbone and enable her to say things her soft heart would never voice normally. 'I don't want to be rude but you are my boss, nothing more, and there are things I don't think it's appropriate to discuss.'

'If I've offended you, I apologise.' His voice was as stiff as hers.

Kim met his gaze head-on. 'You haven't offended me,' she lied calmly. 'I just think there are lines you don't cross when you work with someone, that's all.'

When Lucy bounded back in the next instant Kim could have kissed the child. The look on Blaise's face had been something to see and in spite of her brave words had frightened her to death.

'It's Robert Turner on the phone again,' Lucy said. 'Dad, you *are* going to tell him it's my birthday party and not to call again today, aren't you?'

The mask Kim had seen Blaise adopt so many times had come into place immediately Lucy had appeared; now he was the genial father as he rose, smiling. 'I'll repeat those very words,' he promised, ruffling Lucy's hair as he passed her. 'And I think I hear a car on the drive. Your guests are beginning to arrive.'

People arrived thick and fast after that. Within the hour the pool area and the terrace were full of laughing, chattering children and adults, all seemingly determined to have a good time.

When Kim saw that most of the guests were making use of the pool and that even those who weren't venturing into the water were wearing swimwear or casual tops and shorts, she went upstairs to Lucy's bedroom and got changed. Her anger had ebbed away now and she was horrified at what she'd said to Blaise, but it was too late to retract anything. Not that she would have if she could, she admitted, once she had changed into the bikini and tied the sarong round her waist. He had deserved every word. She just didn't know how she'd had the temerity to voice them and how she was going to face him for the rest of the day.

And all these people! She stood at Lucy's window, looking down onto the terrace and garden. It was true what people said—you could feel your loneliest in a crowd and she had the horrible feeling she was going to stick out like a sore thumb this afternoon and evening. Why had she come? Why, *why*? She had been such a fool.

In the event she found Blaise's guests were a friendly lot. She'd suffered agonies of embarrassment when she had gone downstairs again, feeling positively naked, but as she had walked into the pool area past a group of people one of the women had reached out and taken her arm, saying, 'Hello there, I don't think we've met. I'm Cassie, Fiona's mother. Lucy and Fiona are best friends, in case you didn't know.'

'I didn't.' Kim had returned the woman's wide smile gratefully. 'I'm Kim, Blaise's new personal assistant, so I'm afraid I don't know anyone yet.'

Which was partly her own fault, she acknowledged silently. Blaise had offered to take her round and introduce her to everyone but she had still been inwardly seething at that moment and had swept the suggestion aside, saying she preferred to meet the other guests at her own pace.

Cassie drew her into the group of people immediately, which consisted of the parents of a couple of friends of Lucy's and several of Blaise's friends. It was clear everyone knew each other quite well but within a short while Kim felt totally at ease. This was probably helped by the fact that one of the group, a tall, lean man of about her own age who bore a striking resemblance to a young Brad Pitt, was paying her a great deal of attention.

Eventually he managed to extricate her from the others and manoeuvre things so they were sitting side by side on two sun loungers sipping two margaritas which Jeff—her new admirer's name—had mixed himself. Although, to be fair, he didn't have to do too much manoeuvring, Kim admitted to herself. Blaise was tied up with the barbeque but she could see he had kept glancing over to the group—probably to make sure she wasn't seducing one of his friends, Kim thought sourly. It gave her enormous satisfaction to be able to ignore him and laugh and flirt with Jeff, who was very easy to flirt with, having a wicked sense of humour and the engaging attribute of being able to laugh at himself. In a world before Blaise West, Kim thought she might have been able to fall quite hard for Jeff.

After two margaritas Kim was more than ready for the plate of food Jeff fetched her. A certain devil-may-care attitude had gripped her in the last couple of hours. It was certain she would never get invited back here again and neither did she want to be after what Blaise had insinuated, but right now she *was* here and furthermore she was going to enjoy herself, she told herself militantly. How Blaise could assume she might take Lucy's invitation as an indication she had her foot in the door—or, more precisely, the whole of her in his bed—she didn't know, but she was mortally offended by the assumption that she was here because she had her eye to the main chance.

Thank goodness she had been so careful to give no hint that she was in love with him, she told herself umpteen times as she smiled and chattered and giggled with Jeff. And she hadn't, she knew she hadn't. No, that whole miserable conversation had been a product of his huge, colossal, *gargantuan* ego and she hated him. If only she didn't love him as well everything would be all right.

Lucy and Fiona came to join her on her sun lounger halfway through the afternoon, sitting cross-legged as they filled Kim in on what boys they liked, the pop stars they were crazy about and how vitally important pierced ears were if you were going to have any street cred at all. While Jeff listened in amused silence Lucy begged her to persuade Blaise she could have her ears pierced. '*Please*, Kim?' Lucy's great baby-blues swam with liquid appeal. 'You're with Dad all the time and he'll listen to you.'

'Lucy, I only work for your father,' Kim protested weakly, wondering what on earth Jeff was thinking.

'I know, but that means you're with him more than anyone else.'

Which was probably true, Kim reflected silently.

'Will you promise me you'll say something if you have the chance?' Lucy pleaded. 'You can tell him everyone in my class has had their ears done.'

'Some of the girls have had theirs done twice,' put in Fiona, tilting her head to show Kim she was the living example of this.

'All right, all right, enough.' Kim was laughing.

So was Jeff, and as he bent forward, saying, 'Give the lady a break, Luce,' a deep voice said, 'It looks like you're all having a great time. Amazing how a barbeque breaks the ice.'

'Hi, Blaise.' Jeff grinned up at his host, apparently not noticing the steel in Blaise's smile. 'Great party as ever. And I can't believe Luce is ten. Where's the time gone?'

'On hard work, for some of us,' Blaise said drily.

Kim flinched inwardly. Jeff had already told her he was something of a playboy, having a disgustingly rich father—

one of Blaise's business associates—who was also something of a control freak and who apparently didn't mind his son spending the millions he enjoyed making as long as Jeff left the business alone.

If Jeff noticed the innuendo he ignored it, his smile still sunny. 'You know me, Blaise. All work and no play isn't my style. But I approve of your taste in personal assistants.'

'I noticed.'

Kim decided to enter the conversation. She didn't appreciate being talked about as though she wasn't there. 'It's a lovely barbeque, Blaise,' she said lightly. 'And the first one that I've been to at which caviar was served.'

'Really?' Jeff's voice was soft. 'I'll have to see if I can change that provincial living.'

'Don't try and sweep my personal assistant off her feet when I've only just found her.' Blaise's mouth was still smiling but his eyes were lethal. Even Jeff couldn't fail to notice the chill.

Lucy interrupted what could have been a difficult moment with the guilelessness of a child. Looking up at her father, she cajoled, 'Have you finished the barbeque now? Everyone's had enough and you said you'd come in the pool with us when you were done.'

'I'm yours to command.' Blaise's smile as he looked at his daughter was tender and a knife-like pain went straight through Kim's heart like a spear. His wife must have been mad to mess about when she had a man like him and a daughter they loved. But mess about she had, and whatever had gone on had made Blaise as cynical as they came. Except with Lucy.

Then her thoughts went off in a completely different and

far more carnal channel when Blaise casually unbuttoned his shirt and threw it onto a vacant chair. His jeans followed, revealing short black swimming trunks, the sort that clung in all the right places. Kim looked. She couldn't help it. His thickly muscled torso, the tight black hair on his wide chest, his powerful forearms and legs and not least the way his body hair narrowed to a thin line bisecting his belly before disappearing into the black material beneath had her swallowing hard.

He was magnificent, she told herself faintly. A proud, lone animal that stood out from the pack. It was horribly inappropriate in view of Blaise's earlier comments but a knot of desire had her lower stomach clenching in pure sexual arousal.

'Fancy a dip?' Blaise's razor-sharp blue gaze homed in on her.

What she wanted wouldn't be satisfied by splashing about in cold water, but it might help the way she was feeling. Kim nodded, and immediately Jeff rose to his feet, extending his hand as Blaise held out his. Feeling ridiculously like a bone caught between two dogs, Kim stood up, ignoring them both as she said to Lucy and Fiona, 'Last one in is a sissy.'

# CHAPTER NINE

ALL afternoon Kim reminded herself that the present strain between her and Blaise was as much due to her as him. Of course he shouldn't have jumped to erroneous conclusions about her, but then again she *had* wanted to come and look into his life. In fact, she hadn't been able to resist it. And he had given her every opportunity for a polite 'no, thank you' when he had given her Lucy's invitation.

Gradually people began to drift into the house to re-emerge in evening wear. There were apparently six guest bedrooms used for this purpose on such occasions and it was all very relaxed.

Lucy and Fiona escorted Kim to Lucy's bedroom, and after a shower in the *en suite* the three of them had a lovely time dressing up and titivating for the evening's more formal dance and meal. Kim found herself doing both girls' hair in a cute upswept style, spraying it into spikes and adding some feathers from Lucy's old boa for the fun element. A couple more of Lucy's friends came in just as she was finishing and soon she had a small line of ten-year-olds waiting their turn for her hairdressing expertise.

Things got noisier and more hilarious by the minute and

just as Kim had fixed the last extravagant topknot, Blaise put his head round the open door. 'What on earth—?' he began, only to come to an abrupt halt as he looked at the laughing little girls and Kim in the midst of them.

'Kim's been doing our hair, Dad.' Lucy bounded to his side, her small, elfin face alight. 'And we've painted our nails—look.' She thrust out tiny hands for him to inspect.

'It's only for tonight,' Kim said defensively as he stared down at his daughter and then raised his head to look at her. 'I can comb out their hair before I leave and I've left some nail-varnish remover with Lucy.'

'You look terrific, sweetheart.' His gaze dropped again to Lucy and she beamed at him. 'You all do. But folk are asking where the party girl and all her buddies have got to, so I suggest you scoot downstairs, OK?'

'OK.' Lucy was out of the door like a small whirlwind, the pink feathers in her topknot waving, although the rest of her hair remained frozen in spikes. As the other girls scampered after her, Blaise caught Kim's arm when she made to follow.

'Just a minute,' he said softly.

What now? Was he going to read her the Riot Act for corrupting his daughter or accuse her of making a play for Jeff?

'Don't look so defensive.' He put out a hand and stroked a strand of hair from her cheek. It took every ounce of control Kim had to stand perfectly still. 'I only wanted to say how lovely you look this evening.'

'Thank you,' she said a little stiffly.

'And to apologise for what I said earlier.'

Kim stared at him. He was dressed in dark trousers and a thin silk shirt that had a touch of the Austen era about its flowing lines, and he looked devastating. Sexy and tough and shiveringly masculine. For a moment she was tempted to make it easy for him but then something hot and fierce rose up in her. She was tired of being good old understanding Kim—knock me down and I'll bounce right up again Kim. She'd put up with enough rubbish from the male sex to last a lifetime and she was blowed if she was going to shrug off what he'd said with a smile and a hail-fellow-well-met. He'd been damned rude and presumptuous and a few soft words wouldn't do it.

She raised well-shaped eyebrows. 'What was that?' she said coolly, as if she didn't remember or didn't care. Although they both knew she did.

'I was out of line.' He raked back his hair in a gesture which might have suggested uncertainty in another man. But Blaise West didn't know the word, Kim told herself silently. And then he completely took the wind out of her sails when he said very quietly, 'It wasn't you I was talking to, it was me. From the day you walked into my office you've…unsettled me and I don't like it.'

If she had been able to Kim would have pinched herself to make sure she wasn't dreaming. But that was impossible. She had to trust she was wide awake and Blaise had just said she unsettled him. Weakly, she said, 'I—I'm sorry.'

A muscle knotted in Blaise's cheek. 'My marriage was a disaster, as I'm sure you've guessed, but it produced Lucy and I would have stuck with it for that alone. Miranda had other ideas. When she left she took Lucy, not because she wanted her; she didn't. Like her mother, Miranda neither understood nor liked children, even her own daughter. But she knew taking Lucy would hit me where it hurt.

That and the fact Lucy would be a meal ticket for her. And so she played the devoted mother in the courts and despite everything I did, and I did plenty, she was awarded custody. I became a weekend father—if I was lucky. More times than not there'd be some excuse or other why I couldn't pick Lucy up. I couldn't believe my own daughter was being legally kept from me.'

He stopped abruptly and Kim watched him fight for control for a moment or two. He was still angry, she realised. Angry and bitter.

'My wife had the morals of an alley cat and yet it was me who was being punished when she walked out, simply because she had no trouble in looking the judge straight in the eye and swearing black was white. I had thought I'd done OK when I made my money, that I'd built a world in which me and mine were safe and secure, but it amounted to nothing compared to a woman's tears and fluttering eye-lashes. And so my daughter was taken and put in the hands of someone she barely knew—her mother. I can't remember Miranda even changing a nappy more than half a dozen times and then usually for the benefit of an audience, and she never read her a bedtime story or sat with her while she had her bath or—' Again he stopped abruptly. 'Or any of the normal things a woman does for the child she loves,' he finished coldly.

With a tug at her heartstrings, Kim knew he was telling her he would never trust another woman or allow himself to be put in a position where he was vulnerable. Or, more importantly, any children were vulnerable. Hesitantly, she said, 'Not all women are like Miranda.'

'I know that,' he smiled but it didn't reach the brilliant

eyes, 'but one trip into togetherness was enough for me to learn that when a woman wants something she'll be anything she needs to be until she's got what she wants.'

She couldn't let that go unchallenged, no matter how much he was hurting. And it was clear he still was. 'I think you're being enormously unfair to a lot of women,' Kim said steadily. And yet was it surprising? Abandoned by his biological mother, his adoptive parents killed when he was still a toddler and then a succession of unsuccessful tries at foster homes; it was hardly the best start in life.

Amazingly he didn't argue with her or attempt to defend his jaundiced views. 'You're probably right,' he said softly, 'but that's the way I feel. And when I got Lucy back I swore I'd never go down that route again and I never will. Consequently—' he paused, looking her straight in the eye '—I tend to favour women who want the same things I do. Uncomplicated relationships with no ties. Friendship certainly, along with a respect of each other's feelings and bodies.'

Kim blinked. 'I see.'

'Don't get the wrong idea. I like women, I like them very much. There's nothing more natural than sharing your life and your bed with someone you care about and enjoy being with. But only for the time it takes for the spark to burn out. Weeks, months, whatever. And before any tears or regrets or recriminations.'

Kim stared at him. He meant every word. Her stomach was trembling but it didn't show in her voice when she said, 'I find that…well, somewhat cold-blooded, I suppose.'

Again he didn't argue. 'You're right, it is. It is also logical and sensible. The idea of love sounds good in a book or a film but it just doesn't work in the real world. Men and women get in the way. Someone inevitably takes more and someone gives more. Eventually things become distorted; cracks appear.'

'I don't believe that.' She faced him defiantly.

Now his smile reached the blue eyes when he said, 'No, I didn't think you would. You're one of those rare things, a true romantic. I hope you find what you're looking for, Kim.'

It was like a punch in the stomach. It shouldn't have been, it was said gently and without malice, but that made it worse. She didn't want him to wish her well in finding someone else, she wanted *him* to want her. 'What about Lucy?' she said flatly. 'Are you going to encourage her to go from man to man when she's older? Or warn her not to get married and have a family?'

'*What?*'

She didn't back down, although the look on his face was frightening. 'You've just made it very clear exactly how you feel about relationships. With such strongly held views I presume you'll tell Lucy any permanent relationship is doomed, when she's older, of course.'

'I was talking about how I feel. This is nothing to do with Lucy. She'll make up her own mind about such things.'

'And you really think you won't influence her?' Kim shook her head. 'That's a little naive surely?'

'Leave Lucy out of this.' His voice was chilling.

'She's ten years old, Blaise, and growing up fast. That's how it is today. In a few years' time there'll be boyfriends and dating, and what if those boyfriends think like you?'

He stared at her. 'They won't live long.'

'And this is the end product of the so-called logical and

sensible reasoning, is it?' Got you, she thought, although it didn't give her any pleasure to hoist him with his own petard.

Kim could feel the tension radiating from him and she knew she was playing with fire, but the little gremlin which had raised its head earlier that day drove her on. Why should he have it all his own way?

'Look, Kim, I don't want to argue with you.'

'Who's arguing?' For probably the first time since she had met him, Kim felt sure of herself. This changed in the next moment when he stepped towards her, taking her arms and giving her the tiniest of shakes.

'I'm trying to be honest with you,' he said huskily, 'that's all. There's something between us, a chemistry, a physical attraction. You know it as well as I do. And for someone who keeps work and play separate, as I do, it's both unexpected and unwelcome. OK?'

Never in her wildest dreams had she ever really believed Blaise could be attracted to her. It was like wanting the most outrageously expensive present in the world and then finding it in your stocking on Christmas morning. But she wasn't a child and Blaise certainly wasn't Father Christmas. She stared up at him. Chemistry. Physical attraction. He thought that was bad enough. How would he react if he knew she loved him?

Kim swallowed hard. 'I agree. My work ethics happen to be the same as yours.'

'Right. Well, it's good it's out in the open and we can deal with it,' he said softly, but he still hadn't let go of her and his eyes had fastened on her mouth.

'Exactly.' She nodded shakily, her heart beating so hard it hurt.

'Kim…' His head descended very slowly, his eyes moving to hers. She knew she ought to step back, to jerk her head away, *something*, but she didn't. She wanted him to kiss her. She didn't think beyond that.

When his mouth touched hers she felt the shudder he made and it echoed in her. His lips were warm and firm and for the first time in her life Kim knew what people meant when they said the earth moved. It tilted on its axis and she found she had to hold on to him.

His mouth was moving with more pressure over hers, parting her lips, his tongue probing as it teased the sensitive flesh within. He pulled her more closely against the hard bulk of him and she could feel how much he wanted her, the fierce evidence of his desire both thrilling and alien.

Kim pressed against him, hearing the low moan he made with a shiver of triumph and accepting the thrust of his tongue avidly. They swayed together, and as his hands moved from her shoulders down over the full swell of her breasts to her waist she knew he must be able to feel her trembling.

Her body heat released her perfume, the subtle scent of magnolia and vanilla coupled with her soft warmth arousing Blaise still further. Her arms wound up around his neck as her head tilted back, allowing him greater access to her mouth, and as his mouth ravaged hers from somewhere far away outside their intimate world she heard a voice call, 'Dad? Dad, come on. Where are you? Mac's got the cake ready.'

He shuddered deeply, freezing for one moment before raising his head. 'Lucy,' he muttered, almost vacantly. And then, as he straightened, he stepped back a pace and she felt the loss of him with every fibre of her being. 'Hell!' He stared at her, something almost like bewilderment in his eyes. 'This is her bedroom; she could have come in at any second.'

Kim stood swaying slightly. If her life had depended on it she couldn't have moved or spoken right at that moment. Never before had she felt like this; she didn't recognise herself any more. A flame was burning inside her and all she wanted to do was to touch him and feel him touch her. From somewhere she found the strength to whisper, 'You'd better go. I—I'll come in a minute. I need to… My make-up…'

She wasn't making much sense but he nodded, their eyes holding for one moment more. She could read in his face that he didn't like what he saw as his lack of control. It was there in the hardening of his square jaw and the way his eyes had darkened as he'd taken charge of his passion. For herself she was stunned by the force of her feelings, stunned and frightened. How could she react like this when he had just told her he didn't believe in love or together-ness or anything that made a real relationship with him possible? He had laid it on the line. He wanted autonomy with the pleasures of sex and companionship from his women. That was all. And he didn't even want that with her. He didn't believe in confusing work and play.

Blaise walked to the door, turning briefly to say, 'I'll see you downstairs,' before stepping onto the landing and shutting the door behind him.

Kim stood for a full minute exactly where she was, her head reeling and her legs weak. Then she stumbled into the *en suite*, there to groan as she surveyed herself in the mirror. The swollen-mouthed, bright-eyed woman in the mirror looked as though she had been kissed very thoroughly. Which she had, of course. But she couldn't go downstairs like this.

Feverishly she splashed cold water on her face for several moments, then leant with her head pressed against the cold surface of the mirror as she fought for control. She had to renew her make-up and tidy her hair and go downstairs. People would think... No, no one would think anything, she reassured herself in the next moment. She could hear the band was playing and people were singing 'Happy Birthday'. Obviously the cake had been brought in. Everyone was having a good time and one person wouldn't be missed in the throng.

Slowly she pulled herself together. After washing her face completely she started from scratch with her make-up, brushing out her hair once she had finished and redoing the upswept style which set off her dress. Finally she sprayed a little more perfume on her wrists.

She was ready. Now, apart from a slight fullness to her lips, she looked more herself. She stared at the girl in the mirror. But she would never be herself again. She should have known if she kissed him it would change everything. She shut her eyes tightly but she couldn't shut out the truth. She had only known him for a couple of months but this was a once-in-a-lifetime love and he would never love her back. What was she going to do?

The noise from downstairs grew in volume as the band began playing a rock number. Kim had never felt so alone in her life.

She couldn't continue working for him after this. He wouldn't want it, for one thing. They had crossed a line tonight and they both knew it.

She would have to leave. She held herself round the middle as pain sliced through her. It was the only possible option. It was going to be far too awkward to continue working with Blaise after this. But for now she had to get through the rest of the evening with some semblance of normality.

She took a long, deep breath and straightened her shoulders. She could do this. She had survived the aftermath of David and held her head high during the whole wretched process. It was time to go for the Oscar again.

CHAPTER TEN

WHEN Kim made her way downstairs it was to find Jeff waiting for her. He was immediately at her side like an eager puppy and Kim blessed him for it.

'You look gorgeous.' He gave her a white-toothed smile that was clearly meant to charm. 'How come some lucky man hasn't managed to snap you up before this?'

'Maybe I don't want to be snapped up.' With her heels on she was the same height as him and for a moment the memory of how Blaise had seemed to tower over her was hot and strong. Resolutely she pushed it away, taking Jeff's arm as she said, 'I could do with a drink.

The band was set up in the garden and the tables and chairs on the large terrace had been dotted round the garden, leaving the space free for dancing. Lucy had told her Mrs Maclean was serving a hot and cold buffet in the dining room at ten o'clock, but there were bowls of nibbles on every wicker table and along the bar in the pool area. Bottles of champagne were standing in ice buckets ready for guests to help themselves, along with the well-stocked bar, and it was all terribly informal and relaxed.

At least, that was how everyone else was obviously

feeling. Kim was jumpy and uneasy. She spotted Blaise immediately; at six foot seven he did tend to stand out in a crowd. He was talking to a young couple on the far side of the garden and looked comfortable and insouciant, a glass of champagne in one hand whilst he gestured with the other to illustrate something he was saying.

For a moment Kim hated him. How dared he be so nonchalant when she was such a mess? The flood of emotion provided welcome adrenaline, which had the effect of shooting iron into her backbone, enabling her to turn to Jeff with a brilliant smile when he returned with her flute of champagne.

For the next couple of hours Kim smiled and danced and drank two more glasses of champagne. No one looking at her would have guessed her heart was in ribbons.

Lucy and the other girls seemed to gravitate to her on and off during the evening, and it was just after she'd gathered all the little girls together and taught them the actions and steps to an old pop number amid much hilarity and cheers and clapping from onlookers that Blaise appeared at her side. She had just collapsed into a chair in the garden, sending the children off with a promise she would dance with them again after dinner.

'This is the first time I've been able to catch you by yourself all evening,' Blaise said softly as he drew up a chair and sat down beside her. 'Where's the bodyguard?'

She was hot and bothered and it wasn't the moment she would have chosen to face him again. 'If you mean Jeff, he's gone to fetch us some drinks,' she said coolly.

'Lucy's enjoying herself.' He stretched his long legs and placed his glass on the table, the silk of his shirt, which cloaked the muscled shoulders and chest, glimmering in the light from the carefully positioned lamps wound in the trees. She caught the clean, sharp scent of his aftershave and as every bone in her body went fluid she tried to think of something to say. And failed.

'You're very good with her. With all the children.' He glanced at her. 'I bet all children and animals love you, don't they?'

Just as he finished speaking Kim felt a cold, wet nose push into her hand as one of Blaise's chocolate Labradors laid his head in her lap. 'Most do,' she answered briefly, glad fussing the dog gave her something to do.

'Kim, about earlier. It was my fault and I'm sorry. Hell, all I seem to do is apologise to you.'

'It's not necessary.' She hoped the dim light negated a little of the hot colour she knew was staining her cheeks. She wished she'd left her hair down so it could hide her face. In the absence of that, she concentrated on the dog. 'We both know it was just one of those things; it didn't mean anything. Forget it.'

'I've been trying to but that's not as easy as it sounds.'

Don't do this. Don't flirt. She could cope with his jaundiced views on life and love, she could even visualise carrying on once she had left West International, but Blaise in charming mode was too much. His voice had been low and husky and it vibrated on her taut nerves like someone playing a violin. And that was what he was doing, she thought with a sudden surge of anger: playing a game, enjoying a brief diversion on a lovely summer's evening. Well, not with this lady and not now. 'I doubt that.' She purposely made her tone crisp.

'I don't say things I don't mean, Kim.'

The charm was gone; he sounded annoyed. The dog must have sensed it too because it suddenly made itself scarce. Kim was determined not to be intimidated, however, and she much preferred his displeasure than being trifled with. 'Well, regardless of whether you do or don't, the fact remains that we agreed this…inconvenient situation was impossible. I work for you.'

'And if you didn't?'

The thought had crossed her mind. And she had immediately given herself a talking-to. If, *if* Blaise still wanted her after she had left his employ, it would be sheer emotional suicide to get involved with him. He might be able to enjoy a brief, cold affair but it would destroy her.

'I don't think so,' she said shortly.

'No, you're right. Of course you're right.'

Absolutely. Because when the time came and he walked away from her without looking back she would die. Oh, she might go on living for another fifty, sixty years, but inside she would be shrivelled up and good for nothing.

'The bodyguard's coming back with a very intent look on his face,' Blaise said, with just the merest bite in his voice.

As he had no right whatsoever to object, Kim made sure she gave Jeff a very warm greeting as he plonked himself down beside them, handing Kim her champagne as he smiled happily at Blaise. 'Did you see her with those kids?' He spoke as though he and Kim were an item already. 'Wasn't she great?'

'Amazing,' Blaise drawled drily.

'You ought to be a schoolteacher, the way you are with kids,' Jeff continued breezily. 'Although perhaps that wouldn't be such a good idea on second thoughts. All the little boys would be in love with you and unable to concentrate on their lessons, and all the little girls would want to be like you. It could cause problems. But I'd sure like to be one of the boys.'

Blaise stood up abruptly. Jeff looked up at him in surprise. 'I need to get the buffet organised,' Blaise said briefly. 'Mrs. Maclean is waiting for the nod.'

'Right.' Jeff turned back to Kim. He clearly wasn't bothered whether Blaise stayed or not. 'Ready for another dance before we eat?'

She wasn't. That last extravaganza with Lucy and her pals had worn her out, but Kim smiled warmly. 'Sure.' She stood to her feet, taking his outstretched hand, and walked away from Blaise, telling herself she had to do this in her mind as well as physically.

Mrs Maclean's hot and cold buffet was truly magnificent but Kim found she couldn't do it justice. She nibbled at this and that and kept up a laughing conversation and joined in all the banter and witticisms Jeff and his friends indulged in, but in reality she was deathly tired and wanted to go home. It wasn't a physical tiredness but more of the soul. She needed to be somewhere quiet and, more importantly, by herself. Shortly after the buffet she fulfilled her promise to Lucy and danced with the children when Lucy got the band to play the pop song from before again, but then the music turned dreamy and it was clear Blaise was winding the party up in view of the hour and the number of children present.

For the second time that night Kim found herself alone for a few minutes, as Jeff disappeared into the house in search of the men's cloakroom. When an arm was slipped round her waist she thought for a second he had returned, until Blaise's voice said in her ear, 'We haven't danced yet.'

Startled, she glanced up at him. The hard, rugged face was expressionless but he didn't wait for her agreement, drawing her onto the terrace before she had time to object. He held her close, her cheek against the silk of his shirt, and again the feeling of being small and fragile against the muscled width and height of his big body was intoxicating. Much too intoxicating.

In answer to the warning that had flashed like a police siren, Kim moved away a little, pretending to glance around.

'Don't worry, he won't object to my dancing with you for a few minutes.'

'What?' For a moment the meaning of his smooth, icy words didn't penetrate the bubble of being in his arms. Then she realised he thought she was worried about what Jeff would think. She didn't disabuse him. 'No, I suppose not.'

He drew her into him again and this time she didn't have the will to pull away. She could feel the steady thud of his heartbeat and the thrill of being enclosed by the hard male body was too sweet. She could feel strong muscle and bone beneath her fingers where they rested on his forearm, and as her other hand crept up round his neck her fingertips splayed into his hair, which was crisp and short above his collar. The scent, the feel, the closeness of him was sheer bliss, and, knowing it would be over only too soon, Kim went with the flow. She was going to have to manage for the rest of her life on one kiss and one dance, so she wasn't going to waste a second of this, she decided wildly.

'We fit together very well.' His voice was soft, smoky, and sent tingles down her spine.

From somewhere she found the strength to keep her voice from trembling when she murmured, 'It's because I'm too tall.'

'Too tall? Hardly. You're the right size, for me that is.'

She didn't answer that because she didn't trust herself to. Her feelings for this man had grown too fast for comfort and every minute she was with him they snowballed. Which would have been great, wonderful, if he had returned even a glimmer of what she felt. But he had been very honest. She had to give him that. With Blaise it was good, old-fashioned lust and nothing more.

Nevertheless, she allowed herself to move with him in time with the slow, soft music, aware his chin was nuzzling her hair and that he wanted her every bit as much as he had earlier. His hips moved against hers and she knew her breasts were burgeoning in response to his body, their tips becoming swollen and engorged. She closed her eyes, drowning in the sensations he was so effortlessly arousing in her. What would it be like if they actually made love?

She missed her step and immediately his arms tightened. 'Tired?' he murmured softly.

Contrary to a few minutes before she had never felt less tired in her life. Every nerve and sinew was pulsing with life. She nodded, keeping her head down.

'Why don't you stay the night?'

That brought her head shooting up.

'In one of the guest rooms,' he said smoothly. 'Fiona's staying over with Lucy and her parents are sleeping in one of the guest rooms, and there are three more occupied by other folk, but you'd still have a couple to choose from.'

Laughter glinted in his eyes and she knew he'd guessed what she'd assumed he'd meant in that first moment.

'I—I haven't brought any overnight things.' It was the only excuse she could think of because her brain had gone woolly.

'There are towels and toiletries in all the rooms, along with bathrobes.'

'No, I couldn't.'

'Why not?'

'I'm going to my parents' for Sunday lunch.' That had the advantage of being true.

'No problem. I can take you there.'

'I wouldn't want you to leave your guests.'

'Kim, you've seen how things operate. It's open house when Lucy has her friends round and folk stay, and Mrs Maclean is here to keep an eye on things.'

'It—it wouldn't be right.'

His eyebrows rose. 'In what way?'

'You're my boss.'

'You told me once you used to babysit for Alan Goode and his wife. Didn't you ever stay over?'

'Not normally.'

'But on occasion?' he pressed.

'Once or twice,' she admitted, 'but that was different. I was babysitting the children.' And Alan Goode had a wife whom she worshipped.

'Nonsense. You stayed because it was the convenient thing to do, as it would be tonight. I was going to call a taxi and ride back with you because I've been drinking, but it would mean I didn't get back here till the early hours.'

'You don't have to come back with me. I can just go in a taxi myself.' The thought of sitting in the back of a taxi with Blaise was actually worse than staying at his house overnight. She didn't trust herself not to keep her hands off him.

'I wouldn't dream of it.'

Kim bit her lip and his eyes followed the action. The music stopped but he kept her within the circle of his arms.

'Kim, we're grown adults, not schoolkids, wet behind the ears. It's perfectly proper for you to stay the night at my house.'

Proper it might be. Wise it wasn't.

'I promise I won't creep into your room and have my wicked way with you in the middle of the night. OK?'

Not OK. So, so not OK. 'I never thought for a moment you would,' she said with a poor attempt at dignity, considering her cheeks were on fire.

'So you'll stay. Yes?'

This was ridiculous. Crazy. After all that had gone on today the last thing she should do was to stay at Blaise's house for the night. It was madness. Regardless of what he said, it would send all the wrong signals. And at some point she was going to have to tell him she couldn't continue working for him. Thoughts raced through Kim's mind in a whirling frenzy. Telling herself she was every kind of fool, she said weakly, 'All right, thank you. If you're sure it's no trouble.'

His mouth tilted in a smile. 'Did your mother teach you to say that? It brings to mind a little girl with ringlets in a frilly pink dress.'

'I was never a ringlety, frilly-pink-dress type of little girl. I told you that before.'

'Ah, yes, the tomboy.' His voice had taken on a huskiness that was so sexy it made the weakness worse. 'But a beautiful one, I'll be bound.'

'One with short hair and braces actually.'

'A beautiful one with short hair and braces.'

The music had started again but they were barely moving, just swaying slightly. Kim tried not to smile. His voice had carried a stubborn tone that was endearing.

'That's better,' Blaise said softly.

Kim blinked. 'What?'

'I was beginning to wonder if Jeff had the monopoly on your smiles but that was a definite little glimmer there.'

'Jeff is a very nice man,' she said reprovingly.

'Jeff is a charming little boy who has never grown up,' Blaise said drily. 'Good-looking and amusing, I grant you, but then so is Lucy's cocker spaniel.'

Kim laughed, she couldn't help it. And he was right too, but then he usually was.

'He's certainly not the right partner for you,' Blaise continued, suddenly serious.

His eyes had locked on hers and she couldn't break their hold. They seemed to be drawing her in. A little breathlessly Kim tried for a light retort. 'You'll have me believing you're jealous if you're not careful,' she said with another smile to let him know she was joking.

But he didn't smile back. 'I am,' he said simply.

She stared at him, totally taken aback. This wasn't fair. But then she should have known Blaise would play by his own rules. It was not in her straightforward nature to act the coquette and she answered flatly and truthfully. 'You have no right to be.'

'That doesn't negate what I'm feeling.' He looked at her, his expression unreadable.

Kim stepped back a pace, forcing him to let go of her. 'You have told me exactly what you expect and want from a relationship, Blaise, and frankly it's the opposite of what I would want.' When you loved someone in a till-death-us-do-part kind of way. 'I don't do sex with no commitment.'

He frowned. 'There's a lot more to what I would want from a girlfriend than just sex.'

'But it's what you don't want that we're talking about.' Jeff was hovering about at the edge of the terrace; he had been for a minute or two. She turned without another word and left Blaise, smiling at Jeff as she approached. 'It looks like I'm occupying one of the guest rooms tonight,' she said lightly. 'I think I'll go and find Mrs Maclean and get her to show me which one if that's OK? I'm feeling tired.'

'Sure. I'm cadging a lift with Sue and Mark and they're ready to leave anyway. Kim—' he hesitated '—I've really enjoyed today but—and correct me if I'm wrong—I get the feeling it was a one-off for you. Am I right?'

Kim stared at him. She hadn't credited him with such perception, even though she had tried to keep things merely friendly and rebuff any over-affectionate overtures. 'It's not you,' she said quickly. 'I've loved today, really, but the thing is…' She stopped, not knowing how to continue.

'There's someone else,' Jeff finished for her.

'No, yes, I mean…' She took a deep breath. 'I love someone who doesn't love me. That's it in a nutshell.'

Jeff digested this for a moment. 'Are you involved with him?'

She wasn't sure if he meant involved as in dating or

involved as a friend, but it didn't matter anyway. She nodded. 'To some extent,' she said truthfully.

'Is he married?'

'No, of course he's not married. I wouldn't—' She stopped abruptly. 'He doesn't believe in marriage,' she said quietly. 'That's the problem.'

'So this guy strings you along, knowing how you feel about him, taking what he wants and refusing to consider any real commitment? Why on earth would you want to bother with a man like that, especially looking as you do?'

It was flattering and she needed a bit of flattery, Kim acknowledged ruefully, but she couldn't let Blaise be painted quite so black, even though Jeff wasn't aware it was Blaise they were talking about. 'He doesn't know how strongly I feel about him, to be fair, and I knew he was a confirmed bachelor before I got involved with him, so you could say I went into it with my eyes wide open. The trouble is, I love him and that's that.'

Jeff stared at her. 'Lucky blighter,' he said softly.

Kim smiled. 'Thank you.'

'Then how about we meet up sometimes for a meal or a drink as friends?'

'I'd like that, but—'

'What?'

'That wouldn't be fair to you, would it?'

Now it was Jeff who smiled. 'Kim, I'm not going to pine away from unrequited love, and I'm not the type to live as a monk either. I won't pretend I wouldn't jump at the chance to get to know you as more than a friend if you ever decide to give this bozo the heave-ho for good, but when I said friends I meant just that. I'm a good listener, believe it or not.'

'Yes, I can see that about you.'

'So give me your number and I'll phone to fix something up in a few days.'

She found her handbag and fished out her tiny notebook and pen, writing her landline at home and her mobile number for him. 'I've really enjoyed today and I didn't expect to,' she said softly as she gave him the small piece of paper. 'Thanks, Jeff.'

'My pleasure.' He grinned at her, his young, handsome face open and artless. 'Now I know the score, can I kiss you, properly, I mean, just once?'

She owed him that at least. 'All right.' She had thought he meant they'd find a quiet spot somewhere but the next moment she found herself in his arms and being kissed very soundly. As kisses went it was nice, very nice in fact, but it didn't press any buttons.

When he raised his head his eyes examined her face. 'That was my best try,' he said, half-joking and half-serious, 'and it failed dismally, didn't it?'

'I told you, I'm a lost cause.'

He sighed heavily. 'You're gorgeous, that's what you are, and he's the biggest fool out. But if you decide to call it a day with him, let me know. Promise?'

'I promise,' she said, laughing. He was so nice and she wished she'd met him before Blaise. Jeff was young, rich, amusing and with no baggage, and he'd already hinted more than once that for the right woman he was willing to put away his playboy lifestyle and settle down. But hey ho, she *had* met Blaise.

She turned to pick up her handbag and then found herself pinned by a pair of furious blue eyes from across the other side of the terrace. She looked back at Blaise, indignation warring with unease. He had clearly seen Jeff kiss her and hadn't liked it. And then her temper rose. Well, he could just lump it. She worked for this man, that was all. *That was all.*

# CHAPTER ELEVEN

Most people were beginning to leave as Kim said her goodbyes. When she told Lucy she had agreed to stay overnight the little girl's delight was gratifying, and it was Lucy who accompanied her to the kitchen, where Mrs Maclean was busy loading the dishwasher for the umpteenth time. The housekeeper expressed no surprise at the sudden decision; it was clear it wasn't uncommon for guests to stay over on the spur of the moment.

Kim was anxious to get to her room before she saw Blaise again. Cowardly perhaps, but she felt she'd deal better with him in the morning. He'd had no right to glare at her the way he had but in spite of that she was actually feeling guilty for allowing Jeff to kiss her, which made her mad at herself as well as Blaise. Somehow, in the last twenty-four hours, her world had been turned upside down and she still wasn't quite sure how it had happened.

Mrs Maclean let Lucy show her to the guest room, which was one on the top floor of the house. It was beautifully decorated in shades of pale lilac, green and oatmeal, the *en suite* reached via exquisite sliding Chinese doors.

Lucy disappeared almost immediately to find Fiona and

Kim gratefully sank down on the bed. She suddenly realised she had a thudding headache.

She glanced round the enormous room that was the last word in luxury. What on earth was she doing here? she asked herself vacantly. She should never have agreed to stay. But then if she hadn't that would have meant an intimate ride home in the back of a cab with Blaise, and inevitably…

He might not have kissed her. The argument held no weight. He would have kissed her and she would have kissed him right back. No, of two impossible options this was the least dangerous. All she had to do was to lie low and be out of here in the morning as soon as possible. And she wouldn't let Blaise drive her to her parents'. She'd order a cab herself and then be ready for when it came so he had no chance to protest.

She lay back on the bed, feeling she wanted to cry but determined she wouldn't. If anyone had told her only yesterday that Blaise would want to get her into bed and she would say no she would have laughed in their face. But it only went to show no one knew themselves, let alone anyone else.

After a while she forced herself to start getting ready for bed. The *en suite* held a lovely deep bath as well as a shower and she decided she needed to lie and luxuriate in a hot bath to relax aching muscles. After locking the bedroom door she did just that, finally climbing into the massive queen-size bed the room held some time after one o'clock.

She hadn't expected to be able to sleep, but the events of the day coupled with little sleep the night before had exhausted her emotionally, physically and mentally.

When she awoke the next morning it was to a room filled with bright sunlight and the sound of someone tapping on the bedroom door. Struggling into a sitting position, Kim sleepily brushed the hair out of her eyes. She could hardly believe she'd slept the night through. 'Just a minute.' She swung her legs out of bed and reached for the bathrobe she'd slung on the chair next to the bed the night before. Once it was securely tied she felt a little more in control and padded across the room, undoing the door.

'Hi.' Piercing blue eyes danced over her sleep-flushed face, reminding Kim she hadn't taken the time to brush her hair before she opened the door. 'Did I wake you?'

She nodded. Blaise was leaning against the wall of the landing, dressed in a casual shirt and jeans. She didn't think there was another man in the world who could wear denim like Blaise.

'Sorry.' He didn't sound it. 'I've brought you a cup of tea,' he added meekly. 'I remember from Paris you're not a coffee girl first thing.'

He made it sound as though they'd shared a bed rather than a hotel. Kim was very glad no one else was around. 'Thank you,' she said warily, holding out her hand for the small tray, which held a cup of steaming tea and a plate of biscuits.

'Sleep well?' he asked lazily, coming closer but ignoring her outstretched hand.

'Very well.'

'I'm glad one of us did.'

His hair was still damp from the shower, slicked back but a small tuft had fallen down over his forehead, softening his normally severe style. Her gaze fell to his hands.

They were big and masculine, lightly dusted with dark hair that continued into the rolled-up sleeves of his shirt. Kim's stomach did a peculiar little flip.

'Aren't you going to ask why I found it difficult to sleep?'

'What?' His voice penetrated the liquid heat infusing her nerves.

'I said, aren't you going to enquire why I couldn't sleep?' he repeated, still without offering her the tray.

'Why couldn't you sleep, Blaise?' she said with elaborate patience, hoping to deflect what she felt she might hear.

'Because I kept imagining you in my arms,' he said softly, 'naked, willing, soft and warm. I kissed every inch of you, tasted every inch of you and we...' He shook his head, smiling wryly. 'I was as hard as a rock all night.'

Kim hadn't been aware she was holding her breath until she let it out in a long, soundless sigh. 'I told you it was a bad idea my staying,' she managed at last.

'It was a great idea.' He handed her the tray at last but only so he could lift up a strand of golden-brown hair and let it trail through his fingers. 'You're here, aren't you?' He let his fingers stroke the silky skin of her cheek and slide down her throat. 'You have wonderful skin,' he murmured. 'Smooth and soft and scented.'

Kim was having trouble finding her breath. 'We can't do this, we agreed yesterday.'

'I know.'

She realised too late her mistake in taking the tray. With her hands occupied, she couldn't push Blaise away when he lowered his head and his mouth took hers. Immediately a multitude of sensations swamped her—the smell of his aftershave, the firm, warm touch of his mouth, the feel of his fingers at the back of her neck as he held her head in a gentle but determined angle so she couldn't escape him.

'Mmm, delicious,' he whispered, his mouth trailing a path from her mouth to her earlobe, which he nibbled delicately. 'I should have you before breakfast more often.'

'Blaise…' It was too weak, too feminine, but the waves of heat encompassing her left no room for speech.

'I know, we can't do this,' he murmured, savouring her mouth again before his hands slid under the folds of the bathrobe as he drew her more closely against him.

He only held her round her waist but the feel of his hands on her nakedness caused Kim to jerk violently. The cup left the tray and the next moment it was Blaise who had jumped backwards as the hot liquid reached a certain part of his anatomy. Swearing like a trooper, he brushed at his jeans, the cup, biscuits and remains of the tea scattered around his feet.

Kim didn't know whether to laugh or cry. In the event she did neither. 'I'm so sorry,' she said as his cursing died down. 'Has it burnt you?'

'You could say that.' He took in her stricken expression and grinned. 'Don't worry, I'll live. I might be a bit tender for a day or two but I'll live. Do me a favour—next time just say no, eh?'

'I didn't do that on purpose!'

'Joke, Kim.'

'Oh.'

'But if you'll excuse me I'll go and change and maybe sluice down with cold water. Unless you'd like to come and do it for me?' he suggested with a wicked smile.

Deciding he couldn't be badly burnt if he was smiling, Kim shook her head. 'I'm sure you'll manage perfectly well.'

'OK.' He bent his head and deposited a swift kiss on her lips. 'You wear the sexiest perfume to bed.'

'I haven't got any perfume on.'

'No? Oh, boy…'

Kim was smiling as she shut the door to the bedroom after she'd picked up the cup and biscuits and Blaise had promised Mrs Maclean would see to the cleaning of the carpet. Her smile died as she realised how exhilarated and happy she felt. Careful, she warned herself. She was seeing a side to him that his girlfriends saw and it was lethal. No wonder they queued up for the privilege. It confirmed even more that she had to be strong.

Her thoughts dampened down the brief elation. She had to distance herself from him. He was like a drug—the more she had of him the more she wanted. In twenty-four hours their whole relationship had changed. Perhaps it would be better to let him drive her to her parents' and tell him she was giving her notice just before she got out of the car. But then, Blaise being Blaise, he was quite capable of following her inside and demanding an explanation in front of her parents.

No, she'd stick to her original plan. Better still, she could ask her father to come and get her. If she phoned him on his mobile she wouldn't have to speak to her mother; she couldn't face the interrogation which would inevitably follow. She followed through before she could change her mind and her father, bless him, asked no questions but agreed he would be outside the grounds of the house at eleven sharp. It was now nine. That meant she had two hours to get dressed, have breakfast, say goodbye to Lucy and make her escape. She'd leave a note for Blaise saying she hadn't wanted to take him away from his other guests.

Kim had a quick shower and dressed in the clothes she'd arrived in, glad she'd popped a spare pair of panties in her bag for emergencies. Leaving her hair loose, she applied the minimum of make-up and was downstairs by half-past nine. Mrs Maclean had told her the night before breakfast was in the dining room and everyone helped themselves from covered dishes. When she walked in a few people were already gathered at the table, all of whom greeted her warmly and didn't seem to be surprised to find her amongst them.

Lucy and Fiona came down a moment or two after her and immediately positioned themselves either side of her. Blaise walked in some minutes later. Kim's gaze went involuntarily to his crotch. He had changed into another pair of jeans and a cream shirt and as she raised her eyes she saw he was looking at her, laughter gleaming in his eyes. 'All in good working order,' he murmured as he sat down opposite her and the two little girls, 'although a little tender loving care wouldn't go amiss.'

There was no reply she could make and so she didn't make one, merely smiling brightly and sipping her tea.

As far as Kim could ascertain everyone was staying for lunch, and once breakfast was over most people drifted off to the swimming-pool area. Lucy and Fiona were in their costumes and splashing about in the water when Blaise came and sat at the table Kim had chosen near the poolside. A whole host of Sunday papers had been delivered and everyone, including Kim, was sitting relaxing and reading after the meal.

'Do you have to go to your parents' house for lunch?' he asked quietly. 'I'm sure they'd understand if you wanted to stay.'

But she didn't. Or rather she did, too much, which meant she couldn't. 'They're expecting me.'

He sighed, very softly. 'What time do you want to leave?'

Suddenly she just couldn't creep away without saying something. 'My father's picking me up in a while.'

'Your father? Since when?' He sat up straighter and now he was definitely frowning. 'I said I'd drive you.'

'You have guests, Blaise. I felt awkward taking you away.' Kim took a deep breath. Now was as good a time as any; surrounded as they were by folk, he couldn't object too strongly. 'And I think it best if I leave your employ,' she said flatly to disguise the trembling in her stomach.

There was a screaming silence. 'Is this a joke?'

'No, it's not a joke. You said yourself that work and play must be kept separate.'

'So you're saying you'll see me once you've left?'

This was harder than she'd thought it would be and that was saying something. 'I told you, that wouldn't be a good idea. We want vastly different things from a relationship.'

'So why can't you stay on as my personal assistant, then?'

Was he being deliberately dumb? Kim laid the paper down on the table and fixed him with determined brown eyes. 'Because that wouldn't be possible any more and you know it.'

'I know nothing of the sort.'

'Blaise, this…attraction between us wouldn't make for a good working relationship. Admit it.'

He looked down at the table, considering. He had lush

lashes for a man. Kim had noticed this before. They made her wonder what he had looked like as a little boy. A lost, lonely, hurt little boy. Ruthlessly shutting the door on such weakness, she waited.

He raised his lids. 'I don't agree. It might add a little… spark to the daily routine now and then, I agree, but we are old enough to play by the rules.'

Ha ha. The way he had all weekend? Her face must have spoken her thoughts because he had the grace to look slightly sheepish. 'We haven't been at work this weekend. It has been different.'

'You're still my boss and I'm your personal assistant.' She purposely kept her voice low.

'So all the millions of people in a relationship who work together keep the same distance when they get home? I don't think so.'

'But we're not in a relationship and never can be.'

'Never is a long time.'

Not with you and me. 'We're fundamentally different in what we want,' she repeated patiently. 'Working together would only put a tremendous strain on both of us.'

'I can handle it.'

Kim ignored the fact his quiet voice held a dangerous note. 'I can't,' she stated baldly. 'And I want you to accept my resignation with my notice starting from tomorrow. I'll go as soon as you've found a replacement and I've shown her the ropes.'

'Hell, Kim, you've only been with me two minutes! Have you considered what that is going to look like on your CV?'

He was good, she had to give him that. Kim lifted her chin. 'If you write a glowing reference that'll be OK.'

'And if I don't?'

'I'm leaving anyway.'

He muttered something under his breath. 'This is crazy. I don't want another personal assistant.'

Tough. 'I can't stay, Blaise.'

'You haven't given me one concrete reason why not.'

Suddenly she knew why she had asked her father to come and fetch her. She glanced at her watch. It was ten minutes to eleven. Perfect timing. And the perfect way to end this argument. She knew him well enough by now to know only the truth would do. Quietly, she said, 'Because I love you and it would destroy me. Sexual intimacy to you is spelt with another four-letter word and that's not enough for me. I haven't your experience in that field, Blaise. To be perfectly honest I haven't any experience at all. I didn't sleep with my fiancé before he decided to call off the wedding; his decision, not mine. But I know enough to understand I couldn't have an affair with you for however long you wanted me and then survive afterwards. It might not be sophisticated and cosmopolitan, and I accept there are women who can sleep with a man for pure enjoyment and nothing more, but I'm not one of them. I love you and for me it's all or nothing. Don't worry, you've made it absolutely plain what you can and can't give and you have been honest from the word go. It's just that I can't help it.'

His eyes had narrowed. He stared at her, clearly taken aback but wary too. The cynicism again, she thought wearily. Always there. Suspecting ulterior motives. Looking for an angle. She stood up. 'I'm going to get my things and I'd prefer you didn't come with me,' she said, far more steadily than she felt. 'With regard to the reference you'll have to do as you see fit but with it or without it I'm leaving, Blaise. Once I've trained someone else, of course.'

She turned and walked away, a tiny part of her hoping he would come after her, even if only to challenge her. But he didn't.

Kim collected her things from her room and made her way downstairs. Blaise was waiting for her by the front door, Lucy at his side. 'Dad says you're leaving. I thought you'd stay and we could try some more hairstyles this afternoon.' Lucy's voice was beseeching. 'Please, Kim?'

'I can't, sweetheart.' Bending down, she hugged the small girl, her throat constricting when thin arms fastened round her neck and held her tight.

'But you will come back another day?' Lucy said in a muffled whisper.

She had never believed in fobbing children off with less than the truth, but she couldn't bring herself to be so harsh right at this minute. 'Maybe,' she compromised, 'but I'm going to leave your dad to work for someone else so I'm going to be busy for the next little while. But if I can, I will.'

'Promise?'

'Cross my heart and hope to die.' And the way she was feeling that was a real possibility.

Blaise's face was blank—she couldn't read a thing in his eyes or his expression—and as he nodded at her she nodded back. 'Thank you for inviting me to your party, Lucy,' she said to the child. 'And keep practising those dance moves I taught you.'

Lucy giggled. 'I'm going to teach Dad.'

Now, that would be something to see. Kim forced a smile. 'Great,' she said. 'Bye for now.'

And she stepped through the door Blaise had opened and walked down the drive. She didn't look back, not once, even though she knew Lucy might expect it, but she didn't want Blaise's daughter to see her crying.

When she reached the gates she breathed more easily, seeing her father's family saloon parked some yards away. Surreptitiously she wiped her eyes, and then made her way to the car. 'Thanks for coming,' she said as she slid into the passenger seat, throwing her bag in the back. 'I'm sorry to drag you away from the garden and your pint before lunch.'

'No problem.' Her father's keen eyes raked her face before he started the engine. 'Looks like you could do with one too. Want to tell me about it?'

Yes, but she couldn't stand the third degree from her mother. And her parents didn't keep secrets from each other. Which was good—generally. 'Another time if that's all right?'

'Sure thing.' Her father smiled, patting her knee. 'But you know where we are if you need us.'

He started the car and they drove along the sun-dappled side-road before turning into the main thoroughfare. Soon the car had eaten up the miles and Harrow was being left behind. Kim wished it were as easy to remove Blaise from her heart.

# CHAPTER TWELVE

THE next week was the sort of endurance test Kim wouldn't have wished on her worst enemy, even Kate Campion. Well, maybe Kate.

When she went into work on Monday morning Blaise greeted her with a brief nod and a list of demands that needed to be done within the hour, all of which would take an hour individually. He was in a foul mood but Kim kept her cool, albeit with gritted teeth. At least with him being so unreasonable it was easier to smother her feelings and get through the day.

The next day wasn't much better, and towards the end of the week Kim had to deal with the stack of applications for the post of personal assistant which had been advertised once again. Blaise refused to get involved initially and it was left to her to weed out the definite no-hopers and present a shortlist of six applications for his approval.

Kim would have loved to select six men or, failing that, women over the age of fifty who had been happily married for donkey's years, but she put her feelings aside and conscientiously chose the best applications. These consisted of an ambitious young man of twenty-six, two women in their thirties, neither of whom was married, an experienced matron who had recently lost her husband, a married woman whose children were at university and a young woman of her age whose CV outdid them all.

When she presented the list to Blaise he scowled through it before flinging it on his desk. 'Don't like the look of any of those.'

If it was possible for a six-foot-seven man to look petulant, Blaise did. For the first time in days Kim wanted to smile but of course she didn't. 'These are the least moronic of the lot,' she said pithily, reminding him she hadn't forgotten his comment when she'd attended her interview.

He glared at her. It was Friday night and she had worked late because Blaise had insisted he wanted the shortlist of candidates to look over at the weekend. Kim stared back at him, keeping her expression calm.

'We need to talk,' he said flatly. 'You know that, don't you?'

Kim's heart began to thump like a big bass drum. She didn't know if she had the strength for more confrontation, not after the week she'd had. Controlling her voice with some effort, she said quietly, 'What about?'

'The damn weather! What do you think I want to talk about? Us, you, this whole...' He paused. He was losing control and she knew he hated that. She watched him take a deep breath and when he next spoke his voice was even. 'We need to talk, Kim, and not here. Not in the office. Can I take you home?'

She swallowed. Panic had flared.

With the uncanny ability he seemed to have to read her mind, Blaise said expressionlessly, 'I'm not going to use the attraction between us to cajole you into doing something you would regret later. You'll be quite safe.'

Attraction. It was as if the moment she'd told him she loved him had never happened. Kim blinked. She knew Blaise well enough by now to know he wouldn't consciously do that; it was more her weakness where this man was concerned that worried her. 'All right,' she said at last into the charged silence.

'Get your things. We'll call it a day here.'

With the butterflies in her stomach having a Mardi Gras, Kim closed down her computer, tidied her desk and collected her handbag and jacket. Blaise appeared in their interconnecting doorway as she finished, big and broodingly dark as he surveyed her silently. 'I'm ready,' she said quietly.

They didn't speak again until they reached the firm's tiny car park, which held just four reserved places for Blaise and his top directors. He opened the car door for her and Kim slid inside, watching him as he walked round the bonnet, his face set and grim. Nerves were doing the strangest things to her equilibrium and she forced herself to take several deep, silent breaths, willing the light-headedness to go and her panicky heartbeat to steady.

'We'll talk over a cup of coffee at your flat if that's OK?' Blaise said once they were out into the main traffic. 'Or we can stop at a pub somewhere if you'd prefer?'

She would have preferred the more public place but, sensing he didn't, she said, 'Coffee at my place is fine.'

He drove swiftly and competently and Kim was in such a state she didn't know if she wanted the journey to go on for ever or be over quickly. If he was going to try and persuade her to stay on working for him she knew her mind was set in concrete about that. Self-preservation had come into play. On the other hand he might be going to re-iterate his rationale as to why they could start seeing each other once she was no longer his personal assistant. Either way her answer would be the same.

The luxurious car made the journey far more comfort-able than the train, but Kim was in no mood to appreciate it. She found herself thinking about how she was going to pick up her car, which was parked at the train station, in the morning, and then wondered what on earth she was considering that for in view of the present circumstances. Her mind was escaping into the mundane, she decided, rather than face the enormity of what was going to occur once they reached home.

The mellow summer evening was full of birdsong when they drew up outside the house, the sun casting its last radiant beams of the day over the pavement as they walked up the steps to the front door. Kim was acutely aware of Blaise just behind her as she unlocked her own front door and entered the flat, glad it was tidy and that the fresh flowers she had bought herself on the way home from work a couple of evenings before were perfuming the sitting room.

'Sit down,' she said politely to Blaise, 'and I'll get the coffee. Would you like a sandwich or some cake?'

'A piece of cake would be great.' He sat as directed, and Kim carried the picture of him sitting on her cream sofa with her into the kitchen. He looked big and dark and sexily rugged, dominating her pale, pretty room with his presence.

Her hands were shaking as she fixed the coffee tray and placed a large fruit cake, half of it cut into generous slices, on a plate along with a couple of side-plates. She didn't think she'd be able to eat a thing but she didn't intend for Blaise to know that. Show no weakness, she kept telling herself. Stand firm. He'll try every trick in the book, no doubt, but never once would he mention the word love.

She took the tray into the sitting room and placed it on the coffee table, trying to ignore how the sun slanting through the windows picked up the dusting of grey in the black hair. It added to his appeal a hundredfold. After pouring Blaise a cup of coffee the way he liked it— black, hot and strong—she placed a large chunk of cake on a plate and handed it to him. Once she'd added milk and sugar to her own coffee she sat in the other two-seater sofa opposite him, forcing herself to relax her taut limbs. By the time he had eaten the cake and drunk the coffee she had just about managed to control the trembling in her stomach, and then all her careful breathing and relaxation techniques were shot to smithereens when Blaise spoke.

'Last Sunday, at the house, you said you loved me,' he said without any preamble. 'But that love comes with conditions. If I don't play ball you walk away and forget us. How can you call that love?'

Kim had started at the brusqueness of his voice but quickly controlled her thumping heart. She instinctively knew this wasn't a ploy to get her to change her mind; he was genuinely asking her to explain herself and she suspected past history played a part in it.

This was confirmed as he continued, 'Miranda used other tactics to get me to marry her; she played me like a violin but I was too crazy about her to see it.'

'I'm not trying to get you to marry me, Blaise. I know that is impossible, the way you feel.' Kim put down her coffee cup because it was either that or have the lot in her lap the way her hands were shaking. 'I was trying to explain to you that a relationship between us cannot work, not with me feeling as I do. Your—your other women can cope with having you for a little while, and that's fine; it suits them and it suits you. I couldn't do it. It—it would destroy me.'

'But it won't destroy you to walk away,' he said grimly. 'You can do that easily enough in the name of love.'

'Not easily, no.'

He shook his head impatiently but there was something in the blue eyes that was painful to see. 'The note that was pinned to my clothes when I was left as a baby said my mother was giving me up because she loved me so much,' he said with iron control. 'I don't buy that any more than I buy what you are telling me right now.'

Kim stared at him. Her love for him gave her the wisdom to perceive that this was no fleeting argument they were having here, this was something that had hurt and warped him all his life and it had been compounded by the loss of his adoptive parents and then his disastrous marriage. Trying to think of words that might penetrate the miles-thick barrier he'd erected round his heart, she said, 'Then you are judging your mother harshly if you have never tried to find her and get her side of the story.'

Dark colour flared across the hard cheekbones. 'Me try and find *her*?' He stood up, beginning to pace her little room. 'What about her trying to find me?'

'She gave you up because she was probably thinking

your life with her would give you none of the advantages being adopted would.'

'You don't know that,' he shot back bitterly.

'And you don't know it wasn't the case.'

'Anyway, I don't care about all that. I was talking about us.'

'You do care.' Kim knew she couldn't let it go. He might hate her for it but she had to bring it out into the open now they'd got this far. 'Anybody would. It's only natural.'

'She didn't want me, that's the plain fact. She took the easy way out.'

'It was probably the hardest thing she'd ever done and has done since, and it was sacrificial.'

'And that's what you're doing, is it? Giving up on me for my own good?'

Kim looked at him, at the big, tough man who had conquered the business world and taken it by the throat, carving a place for himself that was respected and admired by his peers. And all the time, deep inside, a small, lost, lonely little boy had been crying out for the most basic of human desires—love. She wanted to reach out to him and take him in her arms and promise him anything he wanted, say she would stay with him as long as he wanted her, be everything he needed for as long as he needed it. She wanted to cry and hold him tight and promise him the moon. But she didn't.

'I love you more than I've ever loved anyone and will ever love anyone again, I know that,' she said steadily. 'If I can't have you I don't want anyone else, and I've already decided to go abroad somewhere and do something vocational with my life. Something that will make sure it's not a wasted existence. But if I agreed to your way of life it wouldn't only destroy me, Blaise. You've already told me your women are like you, they want the same things, enjoy that kind of autonomous lifestyle. But I have seen you with Lucy and I know you'd tear yourself apart if you hurt me, which you inevitably would. You're not as ruthless as you want people to believe.'

He stared at her, his face working.

'And that's why you choose the sort of women you have a relationship with, isn't it? They know the score, they can take it. It suits them. And it leaves you free of any responsibility, any guilt. I understand that. I suppose it's honest in a way. No one gets hurt and you part as friends.'

He had left his jacket and tie in the car and now she watched as his shoulder muscles bunched under the thin cotton shirt he was wearing. 'You've turned my life upside down over the last months,' he ground out angrily. 'I've not known a moment's peace since I set eyes on you.'

'Likewise.'

'I don't want to feel like this.'

She wasn't too keen on being in love with a man who could only offer sex without emotional intimacy.

There was another charged silence.

'I'd better be going.' He waved his hand at the coffee table. 'Thanks for the coffee and cake.'

'Thanks for the lift home.'

They stared at each other and then his voice came deep and resonant. 'Kim, oh, Kim…'

She wasn't sure if he closed the space between them or she did; she only knew she was in his arms again after the most miserable few days of her life. His hands were firm on her waist, pulling her into him, deepening a kiss that was already so intimate it felt as though they were making love standing up. Kim relaxed against his hardness, floating on a cloud of pure sensuality as his hands moved over her body and his mouth dropped to her collarbone and then the swell of her breasts above the neckline of the dress she was wearing before returning to her mouth.

He placed a hand on the small of her back to steady her and with the other lightly cupped one full breast, his fingers beginning a slow, languorous rhythm that made her bones liquid.

His thighs were hard against hers and she could feel every inch of his manhood through their clothes as the kiss deepened to a kind of consummation, flooding her body with heat. Blaise was breathing hard, his chest rising and falling under his shirt, but slowly, very slowly, Kim felt the tempo of their lovemaking change, felt his withdrawal.

'I have to go.' His words were a mutter against her skin. 'Now. While I still can.'

She clung to him, her fingers tracing the broad shoulders.

'Kim.' It was he who put her from him, softening the parting with a last, blistering kiss that spoke of infinite hunger. 'I don't want you to hate me.'

Hate him? What was he talking about? She loved him, loved him so much it made a nonsense of all her earlier reasoning. She would take whatever time she had with him and be grateful for it. She would, she would… 'Don't go.'

'It's not going to happen like this, not with you,' he said thickly, taking a step back from her. 'But I just don't know what I'm capable of. I don't know whether I've got it in me to trust someone again, whether I even want to.'

The torment in his face helped Kim not to fling herself at him as she wanted to. He had come to a crossroads. She could see that as well as he could, and it was one she couldn't help him with. She wanted to tell him she understood but the lump blocking her throat wouldn't let her.

'I have to go,' he said again, and this time she nodded, her face chalk-white and her eyes enormous. Her heart was thundering in her ears and it seemed as though she couldn't breathe, but she stood perfectly still as he walked out of the room. She heard the front door open and then close, and, as she strained her ears, the sound of his car starting up and then roaring off.

He had gone. She closed her eyes. He could have stayed, he'd known that—she couldn't have made it any clearer— but he had chosen to go. She opened her eyes but the room was nothing but a blur in front of her. Sinking down onto the sofa, she let the tears come.

A long, warm bath, a mug of chocolate and a packet—a full packet—of chocolate digestive biscuits later, Kim was feeling not exactly better but more in control. The storm of weeping had helped.

When she had risen from the sofa all cried out, she had felt as though her life had ended. But it hadn't, she told herself wearily. And so she had to go on.

As it grew dark she made herself another mug of chocolate and took it out into her tiny square of garden, sitting at the table and listening to the birds settle down for sleep in the trees in the street and neighbouring gardens. A blackbird made a search for a last meal in one of her tubs, cocking his black head at her in disgust when it proved fruitless.

'Sorry,' she murmured into the bright black eyes. 'But I've got a few problems too.'

Eventually the sky became a dark velvet blanket studded with stars, the perfume from her tubs of flowers and the rambling roses she had trained up the wall enveloping her in their soft sweetness. She found she wasn't all cried out as she sat there in the fragrant night, her face wet and her heart aching. She didn't know who she was crying the most for, herself or Blaise.

She suspected she was the first person he had spoken to about his mother in the way he had; he wasn't a man who ever let his guard down or betrayed what he was thinking. It made her love him all the more but it broke her heart too. She had never felt so helpless. But just because she loved him she couldn't make him into someone he wasn't, couldn't make him think differently. She had seen he was facing some personal demons, scraping the surface of wounds which had been festering for a long, long time, but only he could decide how he wanted to proceed from this point in time. If only his feelings for her had gone beyond those of the flesh, it might have been different...

She lost track of time as she sat there and when eventually she went back into the house she was amazed to see it was close to midnight.

Kim had put on her teddy-bear pyjamas for comfort and thin summer dressing gown after her bath, so all she needed to do to get ready for bed was to brush her teeth and wash the salt of her tears from her face. She grimaced at her reflection in the bathroom mirror. She had never been able to cry prettily. Her nose was a red lump, her eyes pink-edged and puffy, and she looked as if she had been pulled through a hedge backwards where she'd run her fingers through her hair.

After applying plenty of moisturiser to her clean face she brushed the tangles out of her hair and climbed into bed. Knowing she wouldn't sleep, she read a book until the early hours, although she had to keep repeating pages when she realised she hadn't taken a word in. Eventually she gave it up as a bad job, made herself a hot drink, took two aspirin and settled down for sleep.

At some point she must have drifted off, because when the alarm went she had to pull herself up out of a thick, heavy fog to turn it off. Although it wasn't the alarm. Groggily she became aware it was the front door. Glancing at her bedside clock, she was amazed to see it was nine o'clock in the morning.

On her way to the intercom Kim suddenly stood stock-still. It couldn't be. The thought it might be Blaise at the door banished the last remnants of sleep like the sun on morning mist. Tentatively she spoke into the intercom. 'Yes?'

'Kim? It's me. Can I come in?'

She had to lean against the wall as her legs went weak.

'Kim? Are you there?'

She brought her hand across her face, rubbing at her mouth as though it would help her speak. From some reserve of strength, she managed to mutter, 'I'll leave the door open because I'll be in the bathroom for a minute. I've only just woken up…' and then she pressed the button to let him in, opened her front door and fled to the bathroom.

Once inside she stared wildly at the girl in the mirror. Her face wasn't normally this puffy! Groaning, she splashed her face with cold water before dabbing it dry and bringing some order to her hair. When it hung in a sleek, shining curtain she sprayed some perfume on her wrists and surveyed herself again. She wouldn't break a mirror but she was far from looking her best, and her teddy-bear pyjamas weren't exactly seduction material. 'It doesn't matter,' she whispered. 'Just get out there and hear what he has to say and don't, whatever you do, get your hopes up.'

When she walked into the sitting room Blaise was standing in front of the French windows, looking out into the garden. He turned and saw her, a calm movement that gave away how deliberate his air of quietness was.

Kim stared at him. He didn't look as though he had slept at all, his face ashen under his tan. 'Hello, Blaise,' she said softly.

'You—you said you loved me. Right?'

Not knowing what was going to come next,' Kim spoke from the heart. There was nothing else left to do. 'More than anything and anyone.'

'I love you,' he said huskily. 'I love you.'

She didn't move, knowing there was more to this than that declaration.

'I've loved you all my life without knowing it until the moment you first walked into my office, as confrontational as hell,' he continued thickly. 'And that's what scares me to death right now. I don't want to feel like this, I can't handle it, and yet without you life is nothing, meaningless.'

'And it scares you.'

He nodded. 'You have no idea.'

'I do because what I feel for you scares me too. This is a two-way thing, Blaise. You once said in a relationship one takes and one gives, but that's not always the case. It's not the way with my parents for one. They give *and* take. Neither of them is perfect, especially my mother—' she grimaced '—but they adore each other, they always have. They compromise. They prop each other up. They're there for each other a hundred per cent. What hurts one, hurts the other.'

He was listening intently. He hadn't shaved that morning and it made him look even more rugged, sexier…

'It can be like that,' she finished weakly.

'I don't want to lose you.' The words were wrenched from him. 'I've known that all along but I couldn't admit it to myself.' He hesitated. 'It gives you too much power.'

His honesty surprised her. It warmed her too. If he could be that truthful at this early stage there was hope for them. 'What about your power over me?' she said softly. 'Like I said, this works both ways. I don't want to be hurt again any more than you do.'

She hadn't realised she was crying until Blaise said gruffly, 'Don't cry, Kim. I can't stand to see you cry.' And opened his arms.

She flew into them like a homing pigeon. Lifting her off her feet, he sat down on the sofa, settling her on his lap. Kissing her until she was breathless, he raised his head to say, 'This…togetherness thing. You're going to have to show me how it works. It was never like that with Miranda and me. From the start she led her life and I led mine. She…she was already expecting Lucy when I married her.'

So that was how Miranda had trapped him. 'I'll show you.'

He threaded his hands into her hair, tilting her head back, his eyes searching her features. 'I do love you. You believe that, don't you?'

Curiously, she didn't doubt it. Or perhaps it wasn't curious, she told herself, understanding him as she did. 'I believe you.'

'But I'll be hell to live with. Are you prepared for that? And when you take me you take Lucy too. Have you considered what being a mother to a stubborn ten-year-old girl will mean to your sanity?'

'If I can cope with her father I can cope with her. On one condition.' She eyed him mistily. 'I get to choose your next personal assistant.' And the happily married woman whose children were at university would get her vote.

Blaise smiled. 'Anything,' he said softly. 'You'll marry me, Kim? And soon?'

She hesitated. After all he'd said she felt he ought to wait a while. Not that she didn't believe him, she did, absolutely, but he needed time to come to terms with the step he was taking.

'What's the matter?' His voice had changed, roughened.

'Of course I want to marry you but it doesn't have to be soon. Just knowing you love me and we are together is enough for me and—'

He kissed her until she was limp and breathless against him. Only then did he give a choked laugh, burying his face in the soft skin of her neck. 'Don't scare me like that,' he murmured. 'Listen, Kim, let me make one thing perfectly clear: I know what I want now. For the last little while I've gone to hell and back a hundred times a day but last night was the final make or break. I sat up all night telling myself there was no need to change, that I'd done just fine before I met you and I'd do OK after you were gone, but it was rubbish. I need you. I need your strength and your wisdom.

You're my world, the air I breathe. And there's something else. You were right about my mother. I don't know why she gave me up and I never will if I don't try and find her. It might be too late. She might have died or gone to another country, but I intend to use every means at my disposal to trace her. If nothing else I can try. But I'll need you at my side.'

He shook his head, pain in his eyes. 'I'm scared of what I might find, that if she is still alive she won't want to know me or she'll be someone *I* don't want to know. I could open a whole can of worms and for that reason I don't want Lucy to know about this for the time being. It'll be enough for her that we're getting married. We *are* getting married, aren't we?'

'If you're sure.'

'Darling, that's the only thing in my life I am sure about right now.'

He kissed her again as joy, fierce and sweet, spread through her veins like warm honey, healing all the doubts and fears of the last weeks. Then they held each other tight for a long time, his face buried in the silk of her hair as she stroked his dark head and listened to him tell her of the dark and bitter truths that had made up his past; his confusing and lonely childhood, the troubled and sometimes violent teenage years when he had rebelled against everyone and everything, his loveless marriage to a shallow, cold woman who had only wanted what he could buy her and never Blaise himself, the desperation when Lucy was taken away from him…

'Her death made it possible for me to have Lucy back under my own roof, where I could protect and care for her, and I was glad she'd died. Isn't that terrible?' he murmured. 'The mother of my daughter and yet I was glad she was dead. May God forgive me.'

'You were glad to have Lucy back where she was safe, that's all,' Kim said quietly. 'If there could have been a way for you to keep her and Miranda get on with her own life you would have taken it, wouldn't you? So it wasn't that you wanted Miranda dead, not really.'

'You're determined to think the best of me,' Blaise said with a crooked smile, his eyes damp.

It hurt her more than she would have thought possible to see him cry, Blaise, of all people. She bent forward, cradling his face in the palms of her hands and taking his mouth in a long, fierce kiss. He responded instantly, but like the night before when things looked to be getting out of hand he stopped, holding her wrists in his hands as he said, 'Thus far and no further, my love. I did it all wrong with Miranda, I've done it all wrong most of my life. It's not going to be like that with you. With you I can wait.'

'But what if I can't?' Kim wailed plaintively, only half joking.

'That's why I said we're going to get married soon.' He paused for a moment. 'Kim,' he said then, speaking with quiet emphasis, 'I can't promise you I'll be the most patient or thoughtful husband in the world. I'm useless at remembering birthdays and occasions, and sometimes when I'm working time means nothing, but I can promise you I will love you with all my heart and soul and mind till the day I die and then beyond. I will love our children, as I love Lucy, but you will be the centre of my world as my woman, my wife. Those other women, they meant nothing beyond brief moments of pleasure. You do understand that, don't you?'

She nodded. She didn't like to think he had known those other women, enjoyed their caresses but she did know he was all hers now. 'I'm—I'm not experienced like some of them were,' she said hesitantly, suddenly nervous of what he expected.

His mouth sought hers and he kissed her with gentle reassurance at first, then with rising ardour. 'I'm glad I shall be the first,' he said simply.

Kim smiled.

'And believe me, we're going to have a whale of a time when I teach you all I know,' he added wickedly.

'I'll try and be a good pupil,' she said with mock primness, glad they could talk like this.

'You'll be an outstanding pupil because you've got an outstanding teacher.' He gathered her close to him as she giggled, holding her tightly. 'Never stop loving me, will you?' he said with urgent suddenness.

'Never.' She wrapped her arms round him too, squeezing him hard as though by doing so she could take away the insecurity and damage of thirty-nine years. 'I couldn't if I tried, and I'm not going to try.'

## CHAPTER THIRTEEN

THEY were married on a golden autumn day that carried the sweet scent of wood smoke and late-summer flowers in the mellow air. Kim wore a simple white silk wedding dress which fitted her curves to perfection and a tiny frothy veil to her shoulders, and Lucy was her ecstatic bridesmaid, an ethereal little fairy figure in her white and pink dress with its stiff petticoats.

Kim didn't even notice the envious faces of Kate and her cronies, who were standing outside the church when she arrived, and when she walked down the aisle of the little parish church on her father's arm there wasn't a dry eye in the place. Her mother continued to cry at intervals the rest of the day.

'It's relief,' Kim whispered to Blaise at the wedding reception as her mother dabbed at her eyes for the umpteenth time. 'I told you she'd given up all hope of getting me married off, and for me to catch a prize like you! She's overcome, that's all.'

He grinned at her. 'I'm glad she appreciates my virtues.'

There was no female from sixteen to a hundred and sixteen who wouldn't, Kim thought, eyeing him in such a way he bent and whispered in her ear, 'If you don't want me to take you right now under this table you'd better behave like the virgin bride you're supposed to be.'

Kim dimpled at him. 'Promises, promises…'

They were holding the reception at a local hotel, where they had reserved the bridal suite for the night before they flew out to the Caribbean the next morning for a month's honeymoon at a private villa. After the speeches and meal were over the tables were cleared to make room for dancing in the massive ballroom, and as the evening progressed Kim felt she was floating in a bubble of pure happiness. She kept glancing at the wedding ring nestling next to the huge solitaire diamond engagement ring Blaise had bought her the day he had proposed. She was married, she was his *wife*, and Lucy had already shyly asked if she could call her Mum, which had delighted Blaise as much as her.

Blaise curbed his impatience well but, once Mrs Maclean had taken Lucy home, he announced to the few remaining guests that they were welcome to stay as long as they liked but he and his wife were retiring to bed. They were clapped and cheered out of the ballroom, much to Kim's embarrassment and Blaise's amusement, but once in the lift he took her in his arms. 'You're beautiful and desirable and you're mine,' he murmured against her lips, his arousal hard against her softness. 'And I've never known a day as long as this one.'

Kim giggled. 'It's a once-in-a-lifetime day.'

'I'm more interested in the first of many nights.'

When the lift stopped at their floor he whisked her up in his arms and carried her into the bridal suite, which was a vision of cream and gold, flowers everywhere and a bottle of champagne nestling in an ice bucket with a huge bowl of strawberries to the side of it, along with the biggest box of chocolates Kim had ever seen.

She sighed with pleasure. This was perfect. This was so, so perfect. Blaise took her into his arms, covering her lips with a kiss of such hunger that within moments soft curves had melted against hard, angular planes. Giving herself up to the pure sensations she had waited for for so long, Kim felt drunk with love.

They were standing in the tiny sitting room of the bridal suite and now he reached behind her, his hand slowly unzipping her dress. He carefully peeled the bodice away from her breasts, revealing the sexy lacy half-cup bra that made her generous proportions extra-voluptuous.

'Beautiful,' he murmured huskily, experience disposing of the bra quickly as her breasts fell heavy and naked into his hungry hands.

Gasping, Kim arched her back as his lips took what his hands had caressed, his mouth exploring her throbbing breasts before concentrating on teasing the engorged nipples, one after the other. Her head fell back, scorching heat making her tremble as desire burnt a path through every nerve. She moaned, she shuddered, she couldn't believe what his mouth was doing to her.

He lifted her into his arms just as her legs were about to give way, carrying her into the bedroom and placing her on the bed with a gentleness that belied the passion darkening his features. Slowly, enjoying and savouring every anticipated moment, he undressed her, and then urged Kim to do the same to him.

His powerful body was magnificent in the light of the soft

lamps bathing the room in a golden glow, his legs tanned and sinewy. He was already hugely aroused and Kim was enthralled at the strength and authority of his maleness.

His touch was intoxicating as he lingered on every rounded contour and curve, his mouth and hands exciting and stimulating her as he began his first lesson of love. 'I want to kiss every silky inch of you,' he whispered in her ear as a steady warmth and desire radiated through her body. 'You're exquisite, my beautiful wife. Delicious…'

He didn't rush her, suckling and teasing, kissing and blowing gently, bringing her to the point of satisfaction time and time again before stopping and then beginning the whole process over again. Her body was shuddering with yearning but still he continued the sweet torment, exploring every secret hollow, every voluptuous curve, his tongue flicking here and there until she was aching and melting inside.

When he finally lifted her into his hips it was with gentle pressure and passionate control as he joined two into one, his patience rewarded as he found her tightness relieved by the moisture his lovemaking had induced. For a brief moment Kim tensed, but then the tiny pain was gone and the pleasure began to grow to an unbearable pitch as they moved together as one in a rhythm as old as time.

The changes in her body were amazing to her as muscles and nerves began to tense and vibrate with each thrust of his body, electric waves of pleasure mounting and mounting until she didn't think her body could stand any more. Nothing existed, only Blaise and the world of colour and light and sensation behind her closed eyelids. And then, as she felt her body explode in a climax of pleasure that had her moaning his name, she felt his own release and the guttural cry of her name on his lips.

He held her close in the aftermath, stroking and gentling her with tender kisses as he whispered this was only the beginning and they had the rest of their lives to love and be loved. They fell asleep locked in each other's arms in the golden room, hearts, minds and bodies joined as one.

Blaise woke her the following morning by planting kisses on the nape of her neck and whispering sweet nothings in her ear. Drowsily Kim curled into him like a sensuous cat and their lovemaking was slow and sweet as they explored each other afresh.

They had breakfast in bed before getting ready to leave for the airport, their glances holding and their hands touching every moment or so on the drive to the terminal.

It was the same on the plane, and once they arrived at the villa, perfectly situated on a white beach with the sea lapping at the end of the lush garden complete with pool and shade, they made love on their enormous bed, sipping champagne and watching the sun set in a blaze of red and gold which turned the evening shadows into vibrant mauve and burnt orange.

It was a wonderful honeymoon, the days magical and the nights enchanting. They ate when they felt like it, swam in their pool and in the deep blue sea, walked the white sands and explored little towns and villages. They laughed and made love and grew brown and sun-kissed as glorious day followed glorious day. And on Kim's birthday in the middle of the holiday Blaise presented her with a beautiful eternity ring, holding her tight as he told her he was eternally hers, in this life and beyond.

When at the end of the month it was time to go home neither of them could imagine where the time had gone. On the last morning Kim wandered round the villa, touching each object and saying goodbye, much to Blaise's amusement.

He had changed with each day of being married, the burden of melancholy and bitterness which had been with him to a greater or lesser extent all his life dissipating and melting away in the sun of Kim's adoration. She didn't try to change him, she just loved him, and thereby the miracle was wrought.

When they drew up outside their home in Harrow, it was to a rapturous welcome from Lucy and the dogs. Even Mrs Maclean unbent enough to kiss them both, remarking that Blaise looked ten years younger and Kim was as pretty as a picture.

It was the next morning, a Sunday, as they began to open the backlog of post over breakfast that Kim suddenly became aware that Blaise had frozen. She glanced at him and the expression on his face frightened her. 'What is it?' With her on one side and Lucy on the other, he had to moisten his lips before he could say, 'Read this.'

She looked down at the letter in his hand as though it were going to bite her, glancing at Lucy, who nodded at her to take it. It had been enclosed with a note from the private detective Blaise had hired—an ex-Scotland Yard man who had come highly recommended.

It read:

My dear son,

I hope you don't mind me calling you that or writing to you, but I understand from Mr Shearman that you want to find me. I have been waiting for this moment for thirty-nine years. I gave you up when you were just a few hours old, but for each one of those precious hours I held you and loved you and cried over you. I was only fifteen when I had you and no one knew; my father would have killed us both if he'd found out and I had nowhere to go and no one to help me. I knew it wouldn't be fair to try and keep you, you didn't deserve to be brought up in poverty and violence and fear like I'd been, but it broke my heart to let you go. I have never stopped loving you or wishing I could have kept you, but your only chance of a good life was to be adopted by a couple who could give you everything I couldn't. I say a prayer each day for God to protect you and bless you, and each year on your birthday I go to the hospital and leave a toy on the steps where I left you that night. Silly, because you're a grown man now, but you'll always be my baby boy. I don't suppose you can forgive me for what I did. I know I can't forgive myself but I did what I thought was best for you. I got married when I was twenty-one and my husband—God rest his soul—knew all about you and why I didn't want any more children. It didn't seem right somehow, not when a large part of my heart was with you.

I don't know if you will want to see me but I live in the hope you will one day. I shall be here waiting if you do, like I've waited for thirty-nine years. I love you more than you will ever know.

Your mother.

Blaise reached blindly for Kim's hand as she dropped the letter on the table, tears steaming down her face. His own was wet as he turned to Lucy. 'This letter is from your grandmother. We're going to see her today.'

# 2 FREE

## BOOKS AND A SURPRISE GIFT!

We would like to take this opportunity to thank you for reading this Mills & Boon® book by offering you the chance to take TWO more specially selected titles from the Modern™ series absolutely FREE! We're also making this offer to introduce you to the benefits of the Mills & Boon® Book Club™—

- ★ FREE home delivery
- ★ FREE gifts and competitions
- ★ FREE monthly Newsletter
- ★ Exclusive Mills & Boon Book Club offers
- ★ Books available before they're in the shops

Accepting these FREE books and gift places you under no obligation to buy, you may cancel at any time, even after receiving your free shipment. Simply complete your details below and return the entire page to the address below. You don't even need a stamp!

**YES!** Please send me 2 free Modern books and a surprise gift. I understand that unless you hear from me, I will receive 4 superb new titles every month for just £3.19 each, postage and packing free. I am under no obligation to purchase any books and may cancel my subscription at any time. The free books and gift will be mine to keep in any case.

P9ZED

Ms/Mrs/Miss/Mr .................................................Initials ........................................
BLOCK CAPITALS PLEASE

Surname ........................................................................................................

Address ........................................................................................................

........................................................................................................

........................................................................Postcode........................

**Send this whole page to:**
**UK: FREEPOST CN81, Croydon, CR9 3WZ**

Offer valid in UK only and is not available to current Mills & Boon Book Club subscribers to this series. Overseas and Eire please write for details and readers in Southern Africa write to Box 3010, Pinegowie, 2123 RSA. We reserve the right to refuse an application and applicants must be aged 18 years or over. Only one application per household. Terms and prices subject to change without notice. Offer expires 30th September 2009. As a result of this application, you may receive offers from Harlequin Mills & Boon and other carefully selected companies. If you would prefer not to share in this opportunity please write to The Data Manager, PO Box 676, Richmond, TW9 IWU.

Mills & Boon® is a registered trademark owned by Harlequin Mills & Boon Limited.
Modern™ is being used as a trademark. The Mills & Boon® Book Club™ is being used as a trademark.